The Best Medicine

CHRISTINE HAMILL

annick press
toronto + berkeley + vancouver

North American edition first published 2017
© 2016 Christine Hamill

First published in 2016 by Little Island Books
7 Kenilworth Park, Dublin 6W, Ireland

The author has asserted her moral rights.

North American edition proofread by Amanda Growe
Cover design by The Project Twins

Annick Press Ltd.

Cataloging in Publication
Hamill, Christine, author
    The best medicine / Christine Hamill.

Previously published: Ireland: Little Island, 2016.
Issued in print and electronic formats.
ISBN 978-1-55451-880-7 (hardback).—ISBN 978-1-55451-879-1 (paperback).—
ISBN 978-1-55451-881-4 (html).—ISBN 978-1-55451-882-1 (pdf)

    I. Title.

PZ7.1.H36Be 2017   j823'92   C2016-906714-9
                                               C2016-906715-7

Distributed in Canada by University of Toronto Press.
Published in the U.S.A. by Annick Press (U.S.) Ltd.
Distributed in the U.S.A. by Publishers Group West.

Printed in Canada

Visit us at www.annickpress.com

Also available in e-book format. Please visit www.annickpress.com/ebooks.html for
more details. Or scan

ACKNOWLEDGMENTS

THE AUTHOR AND PUBLISHER are delighted to thank the British comedian Harry Hill for allowing us to include him in this novel. Of course, the Harry Hill here is fictional—the author's *idea* of him—but we think the real Harry Hill is every bit as great.

The author would also like to thank Tony Cook of abctales.com, who gave her confidence to write.

FOR CALLAN

1
YETI ANOTHER BAD THING

THE BAD THINGS started happening one at a time.

At first I hardly noticed. It was just small stuff like Mom buying the wrong cereal—oatmeal instead of Coco Pops. Then it was the juice—she accidentally bought bottled water instead. Shortly after that she started reading this weird book about how to stay calm, which had exercises in it that she made me help her with. I had to ring this tiny tinkly bell every fifteen seconds or so while she stared at the seeds on a strawberry and *stilled her inner self.* Strawberry seeds are very calming, apparently. But not calming enough: after about a week Mom flung her copy of *101 Ways to Stay Calm* across the room at me and said if I didn't stop playing the tune to Harry Hill's TV show on the tinkly bell, she'd give me up for adoption. But I didn't believe her: everyone loves that tune.

Still, I went and lay down in my room after that and practiced Way to Stay Calm No. 89. The book said you should not make negative statements such as *I don't like waffles*; you should practice saying what you *do* like. I tried really hard to do that exercise but it was impossible: what's not to like about waffles?

I held on to the book anyway. I thought maybe it would come in handy if the bad stuff kept happening. And I was right, because the very next day, disaster struck.

I was walking to art class minding my own business when it happened. A yeti put its hands around my throat and started throttling me. I tried really hard to stay calm by thinking of something positive to say, but you try being positive when someone has their great big sausage fingers wrapped around your neck and see how far you get. Actually, I love sausages so I tried saying *I like sausages*, but then I started imagining myself eating The Yeti's fingers. (With mustard. And fries.) And that had the reverse effect of making me very, very *un*-calm.

Now, before I go any further I want to apologize here and now to yetis everywhere. They get bad press and I hate to add to it, but the fact is I am being bullied by a yeti look-alike, Eddie Lyttle.

Eddie Lyttle is this great big fat bully who wears his hair in front of his face so you can't see his eyes and goes around terrorizing normal people who cut their hair because they actually want to see where they're going. If The Yeti wore glasses, like me, he'd appreciate his eyesight more. Anyway, never mind that: back to being strangled.

I was very possibly laughing to myself when the attack happened. And no, I'm not some kind of giggling-freak-weirdo type; I'm a comedian. Well, OK, I'm not a comedian yet, but I'm going to be one when I grow up, like Harry Hill (except maybe not bald). So I need to get lots of practice and I tell myself jokes all the time. Yetis don't like jokes.

They prefer strangling people. I don't even know where The Yeti came from. A stealth bully, that's him. Which is pretty impressive because he's only fourteen and he's already nearly six feet tall and he's about six feet wide as well, so stealth operations are a big deal for him.

"Whatchu laughing at?" he grunted.

Why do bullies always grunt? Is it something they learn in Bully Club?

Rule one: Never speak clearly enough that your victim might understand you and give you what you want. Grunt at all times to prolong the agony.

It's psychological warfare, that's what it is. I considered telling him that his grunting tactic was probably illegal under the terms of the Geneva convention. But he was squeezing my neck so tightly that my tonsils were in danger of coming out of my nostrils, so a history lesson was really out of the question.

"Agh, lugh, aah monchk, bachk," I said instead, which, translated from the original Chokingese, means, "Lunch money's in bag. Take it."

The Yeti knew exactly what I was saying. He let go of me, plundered my backpack, shoved my lunch money into his pocket, and trudged off, leaving me late for art.

"You're late," the teacher said.

Have you noticed how teachers are masters of stating the obvious?

"You're making a habit of this, Philip," Miss Franks said.

"I'm really sorry, Ma'am," I said in what should have been my normal voice, but the words came out in this high-pitched squeal, like some kind of high-frequency signal intended to communicate with dolphins and other marine life. My voice is always doing that these days. And that's when the next bad thing happened: Lucy Wells burst out laughing at me.

Girls' hearing must be on the same frequency as dolphins', because they all heard me and joined in, and pretty soon the whole class was having a laugh at my expense, but it was Lucy Wells's laughter that stung. She's this dark-haired goddess who inhabits my art class. I know that sounds a bit sappy and I don't want you to go thinking I'm some kind of pathetic lovesick idiot, but you should see her: she is perfection.

She has beautiful hair and beautiful teeth and beautiful eyes and beautiful ears and beautiful hands; even her knuckles are beautiful. And even when she is snickering at you for being late and getting told off, she has a beautiful laugh.

Oh, yeah, and one other thing: she hates me.

My best friend, Ang (weird name, rhymes with "pang," I'll explain later), is the only person who knows about Lucy and me. I told him about her one lunchtime after I thought she'd smiled at me. Turned out she was smiling at the guy behind me, who's a grade above me.

"Behind you *and* above you?" Ang laughed. "That could prove tricky."

"It's a spatial challenge," I said.

"A spatial challenge for a spatial boy," Ang said.

"Aww," I said, "you're spatial too." And we both fell down laughing.

Good times.

"Philip!" Miss Franks said. "Are you listening to me? You look like you're in a world of your own."

"Yes. No. I am," I said. I can be very articulate when I try.

"That's three weeks in a row," Miss Franks went on. "I'm sorry, Philip, but I'll have to give you detention again. It's policy."

"I'm sorry, Miss Franks," I said. "I got held up." "*Literally,*" I whispered to Ang as I slid into the seat beside him.

"The Yeti?" he whispered back.

I nodded. "He ransacked my backpack."

"He backpacked your ransack?"

"No, he sackbacked my ranpack."

"Your ranpack! That creep!"

Then we both burst out laughing and both ended up with detention. Yet another bad thing.

2
INSPECTOR**CLUELESS**

IT WAS NEARLY FIVE O'CLOCK by the time I got home. I was tired, and I was starving on account of The Yeti relieving me of my lunch money, so I was in no mood for Mom's "School days are the happiest days of your life" lecture—her default position when I get a detention. I really don't think adults should say stuff like that. It could give a kid a very warped view of adult life. Couldn't they at least pretend there's something to look forward to in the sixty-odd years we'll spend not being in school? Anyway, they should say preschool days are the best days of your life because you've never even heard of homework or bullies or goddesses.

And, well, I'm not going to lie to you, I felt like finding my old teddy bear Sir Fluffington and hiding under the covers and inhaling the old days. But I never got the chance because Mom was waiting in the hall when I got home.

She led me into the living room and sat me down in front of a tray of lemonade and homemade cupcakes. Hang on—lemonade plus cupcakes plus detention does not compute. And another thing, Mom had this face on like she was going to tell me something really serious, or worse, something really embarrassing. It looked suspiciously like her facts-of-life face. A face I will never forget. Had she forgotten that I already knew? Please, no. Anything but the facts of life again.

I stared at the cupcakes. They had exploded over the sides of the cups and were black around the edges. Some were iced, presumably covering up a near-cremation. Mom hardly ever bakes. I looked at her, trying to figure out what was going on. She said nothing. She just looked at me in a creepy sort of way, like she was seeing me for the first time ever.

"What's up?" I said, thinking the sooner this started, the sooner it'd be over.

"Nothing's up," she said.

Well, that wasn't true. Something was definitely up. Mom trying to bake was a dead giveaway.

"You're up to something," I said.

Mom said, "I can't get anything past you, detective."

She sort of laughed it, but her voice was a bit wobbly, like she was going to start singing but wasn't ready. And yes, my mom does often burst into song for no reason, and yes, it is very annoying. She opened her mouth to speak again, but her voice had gone all squeaky so she stopped.

"You need to be oiled," I said. "You squeak."

Now, I know that's not the funniest line in the world, but Mom is my number one fan and you'd expect your number one fan to laugh at your jokes, no matter how lame they are. Instead, she burst into tears, ran up the stairs, and locked herself in the bathroom.

Hang on: we don't have a lock on the bathroom door. I'm always going on about how I'm a growing boy and I need my privacy and how Mom is an aging woman and she needs her privacy, but she'd never listened. Until now.

I climbed the stairs and stood outside the door. Tried the handle: definitely locked. She'd done it: taken my advice for once and never even told me. I could hear her blowing her nose like she was trying to blow her brains out through her nostrils. I didn't feel right stalking someone on the toilet so I rattled the handle. Just to let her know I was there.

"I'll be out in a minute," Mom said through a hail of snot. "Have a cupcake. They're whole-grain."

I went back downstairs and picked the icing off one of her cupcakes and tried to think up some fresh jokes to cheer her up.

When Mom came down I noticed her eyes; they were all red and piggy-looking. That's when I knew things were bad. I remembered the piggy-eyed look after Dad left.

"What's up?" I said in my best fake-cheerful voice. I thought maybe Dad had come back to upset her and I was already planning how I could trip him up and knock him out and have him disposed of.

"Hay fever," Mom said and tried to feed me another cupcake. Hay fever? Hmm, that was new. I looked her up and down in a theatrical, exaggerated way that I am very good at. Then I pointed my finger at her and said in my best detective sergeant voice, "I see no hay." I felt her forehead. "And no fever. I can only conclude, madam, that you are lying."

Mom didn't laugh. I was really losing my touch. She looked away and stared at the curtains as if they were the most interesting thing she had ever seen.

"You can watch a Harry Hill DVD if you like," she said.

Mom *NEVER* lets me watch TV until all my homework is done. Something was definitely up.

I usually laugh myself sick watching Harry Hill, but I couldn't concentrate. My mind was racing: Mom had put a lock on the bathroom door, baked cupcakes, and, worst of all, cried at my jokes. What did it all mean? And what was going to become of me now? If I couldn't make people laugh anymore, my whole life plan was ruined: the stand-up circuit, the TV appearances, the big house in the country with the separate suite for Mom. I'd have to rethink it all.

I watched another ten minutes of Harry Hill, hoping for inspiration. When it didn't come, I went off to do my homework. I had to research the Civil War for history but I was too distracted to concentrate, so I just sat at the computer and researched Harry Hill instead. I went through his website hoping some of his genius would rub off on me. Mom always says greatness inspires greatness, so I knew she would have approved. I felt sure that if I could only get closer to Harry Hill, I'd get my comic touch back.

And that's when I had this brilliant idea.

It took me a while before I found an address where I could contact him. There was one address for his agent and one for fan mail. I decided on his agent. I figured he probably gets tons of fan mail every week and it would take ages to reach mine, but who in their right mind would want to write to his agent? I took a sheet of paper from the printer and started writing.

You have no idea how hard it is to write to your idol without sounding like a total weirdo. My first attempt started out, "Dear Harry Hill, You don't know me but I know you." It sounded more like a threat from a psycho-loony stalker than a charming cry for help from a hilarious twelve-year-old boy. In the end, though, I think I did all right.

Dear Harry Hill,
I know you must be really busy with all the TV and home videos you have to watch but please, please take a minute to help me. I am a twelve-year-old boy and I plan to be a comedian when I grow up, but recently I've sort of lost my touch. Has anyone ever cried when you told them a joke? If so, how did you overcome the problem? Please write back because I really need help.

Yours sincerely,
Philip Wright

3
WE'RENOANGELS

I PROMISED I'D TELL YOU about Ang's name, didn't I?
Well, wait for it: it's Angel. Seriously. And it's pronounced
Ang-*hell*. What kind of parents call their child Ang-hell?

"Spanish ones," he said. "My dad's name is Angel too.
I'm named after him."

"Jeez," I said. "What's your mom called—Saint?"

"Encarnacion," he said.

I thought that was a weird name too but I didn't say so
because at the time, I hardly knew Ang. He'd just moved
onto our street and I was trying to be friendly, partly
because my mom told me to and partly because it was
summer holidays and there was no one else around to play
soccer with.

"Ang-hell. That's rough," I said.

"What's wrong with it?" he said.

"It's a bit sort of—holy," I said. "And—um—wing-y."

I never even saw the punch coming. It landed on my
stomach.

Boy! This Ang-hell business really bugged him. And
then just to prove it he punched me again. And then I
punched him back and—what do you know—we were

15

having an all-out fistfight. Nice way to welcome a new neighbor, don't you think?

We were best friends after that. I got a bloody nose and Ang got a black eye, which I was kind of jealous of because a bloody nose isn't that dramatic once the blood's been cleaned up. Whereas a black eye—that has mileage. For days everyone kept asking Ang about his black eye and giving him lots of sympathy and attention. It wasn't fair, because I'd given him the black eye, yet he was the one getting all the glory.

After that, we set about solving the Ang-hell problem. We were both starting at the same school that September and he said he couldn't take any more where-are-your-wings jokes.

First of all, we tried changing his name to Brian, but every time I called him Brian he just ignored me because he couldn't remember that *he* was actually Brian. That's when we realized it would have to be something closer to his real name.

"What about Angus?" I suggested. I've always liked the name Angus.

"Nah," he said. "Isn't that the name of a cow?"

"That's Aberdeen Angus. Different thing altogether," I said, thinking this Angus thing could really work.

"Still don't like it," he said. "Too cowy."

"You could shorten it," I said hopefully, "to Ang."

He stopped chomping on the chocolate bar he'd been eating (without sharing) and stared at me with a look of cold contempt that was impressive.

"Du-uh!" he said. "I could shorten my own name to Ang."

"Well, why don't you?" I said.

"Well, I will."

"Well, do, then."

"Watch me," he said and stomped off to find his parents.

His mom didn't like it. She said the whole idea was "loco" and asked him why he wanted to shorten his name to Ang.

"Because Ang doesn't *mean* anything," he said in a slow voice that sounded like he was explaining two plus two to a toddler.

Bad move. His mom started shouting at him in very rapid Spanish. It sounded like a machine gun going off. She could definitely win the world speed-talking championships.

It wasn't long before Ang joined in and was rattling away with his mom. Then his dad came into the room and joined in too, and the whole thing started to sound worryingly like a great big fight. Obviously, I had no idea what they were saying. The only word I could make out was "Ang-hell," which they were overusing, in my opinion.

I mean, come on! "Ang" is not a million miles away from "Angel." It's practically the same.

Just then, they all stopped yelling and looked at me.

That was when I realized I'd said that last bit out loud.

There was a long silence, then Ang's mom said "Si," which even I knew meant yes in Spanish.

Just then Ang's dad started making this rasping sound

17

at the back of his throat like he was going to choke and throwing his arms up in the air as if to say, "Kill me, I am ready to die." Which was impressive, if a bit melodramatic. He was wasting his time. Ang's mom had made her mind up and no amount of choking to death was going to change it. She pinched Ang's cheek and said something decisive-sounding in Spanish (which ended with the word "Ang") and that was that. Problem solved. Ang wasn't an angel anymore.

4
PEEPINGTOM

IT WAS A WEEK before I saw The Goddess Lucy again.
A whole week! It was agony. Ang says I am suffering from
unrequited love. He said that Mrs. Gray, the English teacher,
read a poem about it last Thursday when I was off getting
new glasses, and that it means loving someone when they
don't love you back. Sounds spot-on to me. And, wait for
it, Ang said that one of the poems they read was about a
girl called Lucy! I figure it's a sign. Think about it: love, me,
poem, Lucy. It all adds up. We were meant to be together.

The problem is, she's only in my art class and we only
have art once a week, but I usually see her around the
school at break times. I'd been on the lookout for her but I
hadn't seen her once. Not even a peek. Maybe she was off
sick. Oh my God! I hoped it was nothing serious.

"What if it's something serious?" I said to Ang.

"You are something serious," he said. "Lucy has turned
your brain to mashed potatoes."

"What's wrong with mashed potatoes?" I asked. I like
mashed potatoes. With gravy.

"For brain matter?" was all Ang said, as if that somehow

proved his point. Then he went off to look for his phys ed clothes, which he'd left behind in one of the classrooms. It was all right for him. Girls liked him. They were always smiling at him and telling him he was cute, even some of the older girls. I couldn't see the appeal myself.

Without Ang I was at loose ends, so I went off to hang around outside the girls' locker room, which is this thing I sometimes do. And before you even think it: No, I am not some kind of pervert. It's just that I have more chance of running into Lucy outside the girls' locker room than anywhere else. She's always in there gossiping with her annoying friend Holly—sneering, unrequiting me, that sort of thing. Last week I saw her twice.

Unfortunately, she saw me too and called me a Peeping Tom, then ran off giggling with her friends. Who was this Tom guy, anyway? Probably some innocent young boy trying to steal a glimpse of the one he loved, and he ends up getting labeled a pervert. Love is cruel.

There was no sign of Lucy at the girls' locker room and I got tired of being stared at by the other girls with that "Go away, you creep" look, so I decided to give up and go help Ang find his phys ed bag. But I didn't get very far because as soon as I turned around I bumped into a six-foot-tall and six-foot-wide wall of a Yeti.

"What are you laughing at, Wright?" he said.

I hate people calling me by my surname. It always makes me want to answer, "Wrong."

"Wrong," I said. "I wasn't laughing." Which was true. I wasn't. I was pining.

"Yes, you were. I saw you," The Yeti said, and pushed me back against some lockers.

There was an enormous clang as my head and shoulders hit the metal doors, and a gaggle of girls came running out oohing and aahing and wanting to know what was going on. And wouldn't you know it? There was lovely Lucy looking right at me and my feet weren't even touching the ground. This was bad. This was seriously not cool. No one likes the boy who is being lifted off the ground by a thug, and whose lips are going blue because the thug's big fat fingers are cutting off his oxygen supply.

Cyanotic! I could just hear the ER staff call out, *Get the crash cart.* (I watch a lot of hospital dramas with Mom.)

The Yeti looked over at the girls, smiled through the veil of hair that hung over his hideous face, and smashed me against the lockers again. Just for show. My head was really starting to hurt now. But worse, this time my glasses fell off and when I moved to try and get them I nearly choked to death in his grip.

"If I catch you laughing at me one more time, you're dead," The Yeti said, setting me free.

Then he stepped back onto my glasses. My new glasses.

I heard them crack. The girls gasped.

"Oops," The Yeti said and turned to walk away.

I looked at my broken new glasses. I looked at Lucy. Then I completely lost it. I forgot that I am a five-foot-nothing, eighty-pound weakling. I charged after The Yeti and hurled myself at him and I actually managed to knock him down.

Ang says this is because I caught him unawares, that I would never ordinarily be able to take him down, as I'm not strong enough. Thanks, Ang.

Well, you can imagine the scene: one long-haired Yeti flailing around facedown on the floor, all arms and legs waving madly, while a skinny weakling sat on him. We must have made a real picture because a crowd of people had gathered and were laughing and clapping and chanting, "Fight! Fight!"

No! No!

Within seconds The Yeti was up off the floor and had me pinned to the wall again. He was just about to sink his fist into my face when Mr. Higgins, the biology teacher, came along.

"Principal's office. Now!" he barked and marched us off.

That's when something surreal happened. Instead of yelling at The Yeti and giving him a month of after-school detentions like he should have, the principal went all soft. On The Yeti! He didn't even shout at him. He told us he expected more of us. Us! I was the victim here. Then, worst of all, he gave The Yeti one lunchtime detention. One measly lunchtime detention, while I got an after-school detention, again. How fair is that?

And then something even more surreal and a bit creepy happened. As the principal was ushering us out of his office he asked The Yeti how his mother was doing. So that was it. The principal had a thing for yeti mamas! Creepalicious. I couldn't wait to tell Ang.

Then I remembered that I had yet another Thursday

detention and all the fun went out of it. Mom would go berserk. And I'd broken my new glasses. I didn't know how I could face her. And to make matters worse, she had been acting really weird lately, staying home from work and bursting into tears all the time. Every time I asked what was wrong she just said she had hay fever. She obviously thinks I'm a total dimwit who can't tell the difference between sneezing and crying. If I told her about The Yeti and the glasses she might crack completely. She was like one of those crazies you see on TV dramas who cry for no good reason, then kill someone. I didn't want that happening.

Especially if the someone was me.

5
THANDTHUCKTH

YOU'RE NOT GOING TO BELIEVE what happened
next. The Goddess came up to me in art class! At first I
thought I was seeing things because I didn't have my glasses.
She wasn't dragged or pushed or screaming or anything, so
I assumed she had come to make fun of me over the whole
Yeti-versus-wimp thing. She just can't miss an opportuni-
ty to sneer. So I wasn't too concerned that I had just put a
spoonful of sand in my mouth.

We were making collages so we had a load of art stuff
out and Ang had this brilliant idea to cheer me up with an
experiment. The idea was to put a spoonful of something in
our mouths. I chose sand, he chose glitter. And yes, we did
check that they were non-toxic before we began. We're not
idiots. The object of the experiment was to see how long we
could keep each substance in our mouths before we filled
up with saliva and had to spit it all out. First to spit loses.

We'd just gotten started when The Goddess came up to
me for her weekly sneer. But you know what? She didn't
sneer. She just sort of smiled, reached out her hand to me,
and said, "Here. You dropped these."

Isn't that just about the most romantic thing you've ever

heard? I was so light-headed that she was actually talking to me, I didn't even notice what she'd set on the desk. I squinted at her and tried to say something, but my mouth was filled with sand, so it was tricky.

"I, uh, Loothy," I said. "Ugh. Thand."

I shut up.

She stared at me. I started to choke.

That's when I swallowed a tiny sand-saliva cocktail. I started to gag and splutter and panic!

What if I choked to death; was love worth that? I imagined my gravestone:

Here lie the remains of Philip Wright,
who died tragically from eating sand
while concealing its whereabouts from the woman
he loved.

I held my lips closed tight, but still a trickle of saliva managed to escape out the corner of my mouth. And then it happened. I couldn't stop it. (The impulse to breathe and be alive is obviously stronger than the impulse to look cool.) I opened my mouth for air, but that made me gag even more and my tongue shot out and deposited a saliva-coated plop of sand at Lucy's feet.

It looked remarkably like a miniature piece of poop. Lucy stared at it, horrified.

I tried to speak, but you try talking with sand in your mouth—*not* easy. "Thorry," was all I managed.

"Be like that," she said. "I was only trying to help."

25

And she tossed her long, dark goddess locks at me and pranced off.

I turned to Ang, who was spitting glitter into a paper towel and laughing himself to death.

"Nice move," he said. "Sticking your tongue out at her like that. Thmoooth."

"Pleathe," I said. "I have thand in my mouth and the Goddeth Loothy thinkth I thuck my thongue out at her."

"You did thick your thongue out at her," Ang said.

"Thum friend you are," I said.

And then we both nearly choked laughing.

Then I noticed what Lucy had left on the desk for me. My glasses. She had picked up my glasses after the fight and I hadn't even said thanks. She was back with Holly and her other friends and they were all fussing around her like a family of demented meerkats—looking at her and cooing, shooting suspicious looks over at me, then looking rapidly away again. Lucy's face was all red and thundery looking and Holly, the Chief Meerkat, looked murderous. They are very loyal creatures, meerkats. You've got to admire that in them. Boy! I'd really blown it. The chance of a lifetime to strike up friendly conversation with The Goddess and I was eating sand like a deranged toddler.

You wouldn't think it was possible, but the day just kept getting worse. Next up was two periods of English. And to make matters even worse, Mrs. Gray was stubbornly refusing to go over the poetry she'd covered last week when I was off. We'd moved on to—wait for it—formal letter writing. Honestly: I'm twelve—I couldn't even go on

26

a school trip to the corner store without my mom's signature. If I need a formal letter written, I'll leave it to her. But I don't like to offend, so I wrote down the notes from the board, which was big of me because I could only see out of one side of my glasses. I had to keep the other eye closed because the cracked glass made it look like I was seeing everything through a kaleidoscope.

I still hadn't given up hope on the poetry, so I looked around the room for signs of unrequited-love poems, but I couldn't see any. There were just posters reminding you what a metaphor is and telling you how to spell stuff. That's when I made up my mind: I would ask Mrs. Gray for the poetry myself. If Mohammed wouldn't come to the mountain, then the mountain would come to Mohammed. That's a metaphor. See, my education hasn't been wasted.

When class was over and everybody else had escaped, I hung around to speak to Mrs. Gray. She sighed when she saw me.

"Philip Wright, interested in poetry!" she said when I told her what I wanted. "What's brought this on?"

That's when I started prattling on about how much I love poetry. I could see she wasn't convinced.

"I even write my own poems sometimes," I lied. "When nobody's looking," I added, to make it sound realistic.

"Philip," she said, smiling, "aren't you the dark horse!"

A *what* horse? Never mind. Just get the poems.

"Well," Mrs. Gray said eventually, "it just so happens that I have a few spare copies. I can let you have one of each. This is refreshing."

Then she went over to her cupboard and handed me a huge wad of papers. She'd obviously mixed the poems up with some high-schooler's fifty-million-word essay in the pile, so I said, "Just the poems, please."

"That's it," she said, beaming at me.

It couldn't be right. I wanted to know about unrequited love, but I didn't want to read all that.

"I'll be very interested to hear what you think about them," Mrs. Gray said. "This really is so refreshing. Come and see me next Wednesday at the start of lunch period, and bring some of your own poetry. I'd love to read it."

Her face had gone all pink and she was grinning at me like I was some kind of prize. I wondered if she might be a bit crazy.

Ang was waiting for me outside the classroom.

"I write my own poems," he said in a whiny voice that was supposed to sound like me but didn't because I don't whine. "You are such a doofus," he added.

"A poetry-loving, poet doofus," I said. "What the heck am I going to do? She wants to read *my* poems. On Wednesday."

"Better get scribbling," Ang said.

And he looked so smug I could have punched him.

6
POETRY THUCKTH TOO

AFTER DETENTION I took the long way home. I had to think. I'd left my glasses at school and I hated the idea of lying to Mom about them, but I hated the idea of telling her the truth even more. Maybe if I just stayed out of her way . . .

But sure enough, when I opened the front door, there she was waiting for me. Again.

"I need to use the toilet," I said. It was all I could come up with on short notice.

"Can't it wait?" she said. "I've *got* to talk to you."

"Sorry, Mom, you know how it is," I said. "I've *got* to go." I ran up the stairs.

Once I was in the bathroom I was safe. But there's nowhere to sit in a bathroom except the toilet. Funny how you don't think of things like that. I put the lid down and sat.

One thing I discovered that day is just how hard toilet seats are. You just can't get comfortable. I sighed and pulled Mrs. Gray's poetry out of my backpack, but I couldn't concentrate. I felt stupid sitting there in my clothes, like a fully dressed person at a nudist camp. There was only one thing to do. I lifted the toilet lid, pulled down my pants and under-thingies, and sat down properly. Far more natural. I picked up the pages again. Definitely better. And that is how I wound up reading love poetry with my pants around my ankles.

This unrequited love business is very complicated. And very long. Seven whole pages long, to be precise. I had to squint, but the type was big enough for me to read without my glasses. I couldn't bear it. All I wanted was a kind of *Handy Hints for Unrequited Lovers*, preferably in bullet point form. What I'd gotten was the complete and un-abridged ramblings of some dead guys.

There were three poems altogether. The first one was by someone called Keats and was called "Ode to a Nightin-gale." I didn't like the sound of that. I mean, a bird is hardly going to unrequite a human, now, is it? But in fact the poem started out quite promising with the line "My heart aches, and a drowsy numbness pains my sense."

Hmm . . . not bad. If I just changed the words a bit . . . I shifted on the toilet seat. "My bum aches, and a drowsy numbness pains my buttocks." Mrs. Gray was always telling us to find parallels with real life in the work of the great writers. I figured she'd be impressed.

I read the rest of the poem, but it might as well have been written in Swahili—I had no idea what the heck it was talking about. So I decided to skip the next seven verses, and as there were only eight verses in the poem, that was Keats dealt with. The next poem was by Somebody Gilbert or Gilbert Somebody. I don't know which, but I couldn't see

any mention of Lucy in his stuff, so I ditched that. Great—
two down, only one to go.

I turned the page and there she was: Lucy. At last.

It was by someone called Wordsworth. First, I thought,
Ger-roovy name for a poet and then I thought, *Not groovy.*
You should have seen the length of that poem. It went on
for pages and pages and pages. I thought the glory of a
poem was that it fit on one page. I was feeling seriously
swindled, but I read the first line anyway. "Strange fits of
passion have I known ..."

Wow! That bit really spoke to me, because I did once
have a coughing fit in the lunchroom when Lucy sat down
opposite me and I was so lovestruck that my mango and
pomegranate smoothie went down the wrong way and
nearly killed me.

The rest of the poem did not speak to me—or, if it did,
I had no idea what it was saying. As far as I could make
out, some guy rides past his girlfriend's house one moonlit
night and thinks, *OMG! What if she's, like, dead?* I was
beginning to think maybe Wordsworth wasn't very bright.
I mean, who goes around imagining their girlfriend is dead
for no good reason? But then I read these lines:

I to her cottage bent my way
Beneath an evening moon.

Now, I don't know about you, but I call that stalking.
If I crept over to Lucy's house in the moonlight and hung
around outside her window, she'd probably have me arrested. And another thing. Wordsworth needed to learn how

to write a sentence. If in language back to front wrote I, the teacher kill me would. And it kept getting worse because the more I read, the less I understood, and my buttocks felt like they were glued to the toilet seat and were starting to get a bit numb, and Mrs. Gray was going to ask me all about it (the poetry, not my butt) and ... *Help!*

Just then my cell rang. It was Ang. What do you know? You just have to call out for help and help comes!

"You're psychic," I said.

"Am I?" he said, sounding surprised. "You'd think I'd know that much, then."

He was eating chips. I could tell by the deafening crunch. Food is the love of Ang's life. I didn't say too much about it before because he's self-conscious about his weight and I don't like to draw attention to it. I thought I could hear Mom outside the door again, so I lowered my voice.

"I need your help," I whispered to Ang.

"Why are you whispering?" he asked.

"Because I'm on the toilet."

"Blech!" he groaned. "You've put me off my chips."

"Ang," I pleaded, "you've got to help me."

"You want me to come and rescue you from the toilet?"

"Poetry sucks," I said, trying to ignore his chomping.

"What do you want me to do about it?" Ang mumbled through his chips.

"Explain it," I said.

"How should I know?" Ang said. "I'm no poet."

"You were there that day in class."

32

"So? I was there when I was born, but I don't remember any of that."

You can't argue with logic like that, so I didn't argue.

"You said this Lucy poem was good," I said accusingly.

"No, I never. I said it was about someone called Lucy."

"Ang, you told me it was about unrequited love."

"No, I didn't. I said we did a poem about unrequited love and that we did a poem about someone called Lucy. I don't know which is which. We did another poem too but I can't remember what it was about."

"Sore buttocks," I said.

"Really? You'd think I'd remember that."

I was starting to think maybe Ang knew as little about the poems as I did.

"Listen," I said. "Finish your chips and focus. What is the Lucy poem about?"

"Dunno."

"Try! This is important."

"OK." Ang swallowed loudly. "I *think* Mrs. Gray said Wordsworth wrote this poem about nature or love or something. And that he was obsessed with Lucy, but that she might be a figment of his imagination or an idea or something."

An idea! "You mean Lucy wasn't even real?" That's when I lost all respect for Wordsworth. I mean, who invents girlfriends that might possibly be ideas for themselves? I could hear Ang munching away on his chips again without a care in the world, and I wanted to throttle him. Maybe he'd gotten it wrong. "God, Ang! *Concentrate*," I squawked. "Help meeee!"

I must have shouted that last bit because Mom came thundering up the stairs and started banging on the door. I was so startled I nearly peed myself. Which wasn't really a problem because I was sitting on the toilet, but still, you like to be in full control of your bladder.

"Philip? Are you all right?" she said through the door. Her voice was all panicky.

Seriously, what did she think could happen to me sitting on the toilet?

"Let me in," she squawked.

Let me remind you: I am twelve years old, nearly thirteen. I do not need help with my toilet activities.

"Go away!" I hissed at her.

"Be like that," Ang said, all huffy.

"Not you," I explained. "Her."

"Her?" Ang squawked. "Have you got a girl in there with you?"

"Shut up, you pervert!" It was my turn to squawk.

"Don't you speak to me like that," Mom cried. "You come out here right now."

"I'm sorry," I said. "I didn't mean you."

But she wouldn't listen. She started banging on the door again.

"Go away!" I yelled.

"That's it," Ang said. "I've had enough." But he didn't hang up.

Just then, Mom began to cry. Real, big, choky sobs. "I didn't bring you up to talk to me like that," she wailed. "I'm under a lot of stress right now," she sobbed. "I need your help and ..." (sob) "... your love." And then she blew her nose. It sounded like an elephant being slaughtered.

"I'm sorry," I said. "You know I love you."

"You what!" Ang screeched down the phone.

"Not you, you creep," I said.

"Who are you calling a creep?" Mom said, and started bawling all over again.

I was thinking the only way out of the situation would be to put my head down the toilet and flush, when the doorbell rang.

"Who's that?" Mom said, sounding a bit panicked.

"How the heck should I know? In case you hadn't noticed, *I am on the toilet!*"

The doorbell rang again and the person outside lifted the letter flap.

"Yoo-hoo! Kathy, let me in," the person cooed. "I come bearing gifts."

It was Susie, Mom's best friend. Hallelujah. Mom blew her nose again and went down to let her in.

I picked up my phone and said to Ang, "Now, about Wordsworth ..."

But he was gone.

7
HAIRFRIGHTENER

ONCE I KNEW it was Susie down there, I knew it would
be safe to come out. She always puts Mom in a good mood.
I bolted down the stairs, then walked calmly into the living
room, trying not to look like someone who indulged in
bare-bum poetry recitals. Mom and Susie stopped talking
when they saw me.

"How's my favorite comedian?" Susie said.

"What do you call a man with a seagull on his head?" I
asked her.

"Cliff," she said. "You'll have to do better than that."

"OK," I said, rising to the challenge. "What do you call a
man with bananas in both ears?"

"Haven't you got homework to do?" Mom said, interrupting me. Mom is very keen on homework.

"Wait," Susie said, "until your mom opens her presents."

"Presents?" I said dumbly, like I'd never heard the word
before.

"Presents?" Mom said, like she was trying to outdo me
in the stupid stakes.

"Pres-ents," Susie said, like she was translating at a
National Institute for Idiots Convention. "You know, gifts

wrapped in paper, given on special occasions." And she handed over a bag to Mom. "Belated happy birthday to you," she sang. "Happy birthday, dear Kathy, happy birthday to you."

"That was a month ago," Mom said.

"So? I was away. Open!"

Mom removed a bottle-shaped present from the bag, which, when unwrapped, turned out to be a bottle. Full of her favorite wine. Mom smiled. Good old Susie. Mom loves presents. She lifted a longish, rectangular box from the bag. It looked like it might contain a new controller for my game console. I grinned. Mom grinned—all traces of the dreaded piggy eyes gone.

Susie had obviously put quite an effort into the wrapping because there was a lot of tape on it and Mom had to bite at it with her teeth. So there was Mom, grinning and gnawing away at her present as happy as a beaver with a log, and for the first time in a week I felt like things were normal again. Not that my mother going around gnawing things is the norm; I just mean she had stopped being serious for half a second and whatever it was that was bothering her vanished.

"Careful," Susie said. "I don't want to have to pay for replacement dentures!"

Mom laughed and eventually managed to tear off the paper. "A hair straightener!" she announced.

Not the most exciting present in the world, I think you'll agree. I have to admit I was a teensy bit disappointed, but I kept on grinning, just for show. Anyway, Mom would be happy. She'd been talking about getting a hair straightener for ages.

But you know what she did? She burst into tears and ran out of the room and up the stairs and locked herself in the bathroom.

Susie and I looked at each other. We could hear Mom sobbing.

"Why don't you go over to Ang's?" Susie suggested.

And even though my mom was locked in a bathroom bawling like a baby, I thought, *Cool.* I never get to go to Ang's on a weeknight because of homework.

I was out the door like a shot.

8
HA-LUCY-NATIONS

ON THE WAY OVER to Ang's, I called to let him know I was coming.

"On a weeknight?" he asked. "Has your mother lost her mind?"

How did he know?

"It's a treat for her birthday," I lied. I didn't want him to know that my mother had, in fact, lost her mind and was locked in the bathroom because she had developed a sudden and worrying fear of hairstyling equipment. "Can I come over or can't I?"

"OK," Ang said. "But no poetry and no telling me you love me. Deal?"

"Deal," I said.

As I was stuffing my phone back into my pocket, I noticed a girl in a blue hoodie standing at the corner of the street who looked remarkably like Lucy. I can honestly say that was the first time I really missed my glasses. I could cope with not being able to see the board at school, no sweat, but now I couldn't even bring the love of my life into focus. The weird thing is, Lucy doesn't live anywhere near me and she is a complete keener so there was no chance she'd be out on a weeknight. There was only one possible explanation: I was hallucinating. Ha-Lucy-nating, to be precise. See what love does to you? It makes you mentally deranged.

Still, even a hallucination of Lucy was better than nothing and I couldn't help thinking, *If only she were mine*. I sat on the wall outside Ang's house to let the thought sink in and before I knew it, I'd composed a poem about her. I think you'll agree that writing a poem based on a hallucination of a girl who didn't even love me in the first place shows great skill and imagination. But even though I'd actually succeeded in composing a poem, I still felt a bit sick to my stomach. Because, the truth is—I meant that poem. And I knew I'd have to write it down quickly or I'd forget it, so I got up and rang Ang's doorbell.

His mom greeted me by patting me on the head and pinching my cheek like I was a cross between a Labrador and a toddler. I must really be adorable to have this effect on her. She smiled at me as she walked me to Ang's room and said something in Spanish before leaving.

"What did she say?" I asked Ang, who was sitting at his computer.

"*Donde hay amor, hay dolor*," he said without turning around.

"In English, please," I said.

"It's a Spanish proverb," Ang said. "It means where there is love, there is pain."

"You told her!" I squawked.

"Told her what? There's nothing to tell."

"About Lucy."

"Are you nuts?" Ang said. "I don't have to tell her anything. You've got it written all over your face. You're like a big, miserable bloodhound."

"Bloodhound, really?" I said. "I was thinking more—cuddly Labrador."

"Poodle," Ang said.

"Shut up. I am not a poodle."

And then we started making dog noises, howling and barking and performing dog tricks until I remembered I wasn't a dog, I was a poet, and I needed to write my poem down before I forgot it.

"Sit," I said.

Ang sat. Maybe I'll become a dog trainer when I grow up. "Type this up," I said, but he ignored me this time. "Quick, before I forget."

"I'm not your slave," Ang said, staring at his computer.

He can be seriously stubborn when he wants. "Do you have paper in the printer?"

"Hmm?" he said, scanning some girl's Facebook page.

"*A-ang!*" I pleaded. "This is a matter of life and death."

He stopped staring at the computer and swiveled around to look at me.

"Whose life or death?" he asked.

"Mine," I said, and before he had time to turn back to his computer I added, "I did it. I wrote a love poem for Mrs. Gray."

"For Mrs. Gray! Are you in love with *her* now?"

"No, you freak. It's *about* Lucy, but it's *for* Mrs. Gray."

"You're going to give your Lucy love poem to Mrs. Gray?" Ang said, looking worried. "Don't you think that'll send her the wrong kind of message?"

"Oh, hilarious," I said. "She thinks I'm a poet, remember? Come on, it'll only take a minute."

Ang groaned but turned to the keyboard. "I said no poetry, but OK, go!" he said.

I cleared my throat and announced, "If she were mine." I paused for dramatic effect.

Ang turned around. "Is that it?"

"That," I said scornfully, "is the title."

Then I recited the whole poem from start to finish and Ang rattled away on the keyboard, and he didn't even snort or scoff once—told you it was good. When he was finished typing, he printed off a copy and we both stared at the finished product:

> *If she were mine*
> *My eyes would shine.*
> *I'd sing out loud*
> *And be so proud.*
> *If she were mine*
> *It'd be so fine.*
> *I'd dance around*
> *And pet a hound.*
> *If she were mine I wouldn't stalk*
> *I'd go right up and talk.*
> *If she were mine.*

"That is *so* lame," Ang said.

"*That* is my soul you're talking about," I said.

"Anyway," Ang said, "don't poems have to be all weird, and not be about what they're really about? And don't you have to use weird language like *thee* and *thou*?"

"I'm writing a poem," I said, "not time-traveling."

Ang handed me the poem. "What's the big rush, anyway?" he said. "I thought you had until next Wednesday."

"Trust me, you don't want to know," I said.

"Go on," Ang said. "You know you want to tell me."

How did he know that? I was beginning to think that maybe Ang really was psychic.

"I won't have time next week," I confessed. "I think my mother is having a breakdown, so I'll be busy next week visiting her in a high-security mental hospital."

"Wow!" Ang said. "What are the signs?"

"She bakes and cries a lot."

"No way! So does mine." He looked delighted. I could tell he wasn't taking this seriously.

"Do you think my mom might be crazy too?" he asked.

I gave this some thought, then concluded, "If she is, she's crazy all the time because she hasn't changed, which means she's normal-crazy because that's normal for her."

"Normal-crazy?"

"Yes," I said decisively, "but *my* mom normally buys cakes from the store and normally laughs like a hyena all of the time. So this baking and crying business is really abnormal and means that she is worryingly crazy."

"I see," said Ang. And I thought maybe he did see

because he looked very serious. Then he said, "They'll have to lock her up, away from any baking utensils, in case she tries to harm herself with a spatula."

"Oh. My. God," I said. "A spatula attack. That alone is probably a criminal offense."

"High risk," Ang added. "Category A."

"High-security unit for sure," I said. "With guard dogs and barbed-wire fences in case she tries to dig her way out with a wooden spoon and bake some cupcakes."

"Or muffins," Ang suggested.

"Brownies."

"Squares," Ang said with tears in his eyes.

And we both fell over laughing and shouting out the names of all the cakes we could think of.

After that I felt a whole lot better.

But on my way back home I saw my Ha-Lucy-nation again, and this time it was talking to another person in a hoodie. And the other hoodied person was a boy. Oh my God! My hallucination was cheating on me.

I was immediately plunged into despair. It's true what they say: love really is a roller coaster of emotion. One minute you're all smiles, writing poetry, and the next you're miserable and considering beating up the hallucination that is talking to your imaginary girlfriend. It would wear you out.

This is not how I imagined love would be. Once when I was watching a sappy movie with Mom about a boy who finds comfort in his first love after his dog dies (the dog bit was good), Mom said to me, "Just you wait until you fall in love. It will be so wonderful." Shows you how much she knows. Maybe back in the old days when Mom was in love, things were different. Back then girls probably wore pigtails, and boys carried their backpacks home from school. Well, things are different in the modern world. Just supposing Lucy would even let me near her backpack, do you know how much the average backpack weighs now? If I were to attempt to carry both our backpacks home from school, I'd end up with severe curvature of the spine, and then I'd be a five-foot-nothing, eighty-pound, four-eyed guy with a stoop.

Take it from me: modern love is hell.

9
INSOMNIA

SUSIE MET ME at the front door.

"Aww," she said, "what's wrong? Do you want a hug?"

Being in love was bad, but it wasn't that bad.

"*No way!*" I said, pushing past her.

"Ouch!" Susie said. She looked a bit hurt. That's when I noticed her eyes were really red. So she had developed pig-eye syndrome too. It must be contagious.

"Come on," she said. "Cheer up and have some fries. I can't cope with two Wrights being wrong."

Get it? Two Wrights—me and Mom. That's an old joke of Susie's that I usually pretend to find funny, but this time I didn't have the heart.

"What's wrong with the other Wright?" I said, stuffing my mouth with fries.

"She's in bed," Susie said. "She's really not feeling very well, so she's having a sleep." Then she added, "And don't talk with your mouth full. It's beyond revolting."

Adults are unbelievable. My mom was possibly mentally unstable, and all Susie could think about was my table manners.

"Can I go up and see her?" I asked. "After I eat?"

"She's worn out, Philip. I think we should let her sleep."

"What's wrong with her?" I asked again. "She's been acting really weird."

Susie choked on one of her fries, then said, "Oh, I forgot. Your mom said you could watch one of your Harry Hill DVDs and eat your dinner off your knees tonight."

"Then what are we waiting for?" I said.

Susie stayed until I'd finished my homework and had my shower and was supposedly ready for bed. I tried telling her I didn't usually go to bed until midnight, but she wouldn't listen. She made me go to bed at nine thirty and checked that I had her phone number in my cell. She told me to keep it on and phone her if we needed anything.

"Mom doesn't let me keep my phone on at night," I told her.

"And you always do what Mom says, do you?"

"She says I'll get brain damage or head cancer or something," I said.

"Oh!" Susie said. "Well, in that case, just switch it on if you need me."

She looked a bit flustered, but I didn't really think she should take that stuff too seriously. I think Mom just made it up to stop me from using my phone at night.

After Susie let herself out, I went into Mom's room to see how she was, but she was fast asleep with the light off so I went back to my own room and got into bed. Nine thirty-five: I had a long night ahead of me.

By midnight I must have counted over two million sheep, and I'd decided that I definitely do not want to be a sheep farmer when I grow up. It looks glamorous on those Australian documentaries, but when you've spent hours in bed with millions of sheep, the glamour kinda wears thin.

At two a.m. I crept out of bed and into Mom's room; she was still asleep. I could tell because apart from the closed eyes and the lifeless body, she was snoring a bit. There was a box of pills on her bedside table. They were new. I tried to see what was on the label, but it was too dark. Probably vitamins. Mom's always going on about vitamins.

I stood in her doorway and made another discovery: your house is a very lonely place when you're the only one awake. I didn't like this discovery. It led to a very unsettling train of thought: The Yeti and my broken glasses and detention and Mrs. Gray's poetry and Lucy.

And my feet were cold.

If Mom had been awake she'd have cheered me up. I stood there in the dark remembering how, when I was small and couldn't sleep, she used to get my teddy bear Sir Fluffington and cuddle me back into bed. Those days were long over, and now Mom was going crazy. I shivered. Poor Mom. That's when I decided to give in to the temptation to write to Harry Hill again. I didn't want to pester him or look like a stalker who doesn't even wait for a reply in between letters, but I was desperate.

Dear Harry Hill,
You haven't had time to reply to my first letter
yet, but I just thought I would update you on
what's been happening. My mom only has to
look at me now and she bursts into tears. She
doesn't even wait to find out if my joke will be
any good. I'm getting desperate. Please advise.

Yours sincerely,
Philip Wright

PS: I know it's not your area of expertise,
but if you have any hints on dealing with unrequited love or advice on writing poetry, I'd
really appreciate it.

10
CLEANCRAZY

I HEARD THE SOUND of vacuuming. I checked my watch and saw that it was only six thirty a.m., so I figured I had to be dreaming. My mother has many faults, but cleaning the house at the crack of dawn is not one of them.

"Dammit!" I heard Mom say to the vacuum cleaner. "Work properly, won't you?"

So I wasn't dreaming.

"It can't understand you," I called out. "It's an inanimate object."

I dragged myself downstairs. "What are you doing?" I yawned.

"Cleaning," she said.

"Du-uh!" I said. "But why now, at six o'clock in the morning?"

"Don't exaggerate, Philip," she said. "It's already past six thirty." She sounded really snappy.

I decided to put the kettle on. Maybe if I made her a cup of tea she'd sit down and tell me what was going on. Maybe we were going on vacation. Mom always cleans the house from top to bottom before we go on vacation. She likes to leave it nice and clean for the burglars. I wondered where we were going. Somewhere warm, I bet. Mom loves the sun.

After I'd put the kettle on, I planned on lining up all the cereal boxes on the table and reading the backs of them. But then I remembered I had no glasses. You see the ripple effect of The Yeti's actions? Chaos theory.

I said I liked to line up *all* the cereal boxes, but these days it's usually just two: muesli and rolled oats (which is really just muesli with the muesli taken out). Mom has become a bit of a health nut when it comes to food and stuff. She's become obsessed with eating five vegetables a day and not eating foods that contain sugar and salt and trans fats, whatever they are. Mom is also obsessed with switching off cell phones and the Wi-Fi and making me walk places when I could just as easily take a bus. Now she had developed a new obsession: early-morning cleaning. I made the tea, then sat down to my cereal and watched her.

"Have some tea," I said.

"No time," she said. "This place is filthy."

"It'll still be filthy when you've had your tea," I said cheerfully.

"Oh, ha ha! Mr. Goddamn Comedian," Mom said in this really ugly voice. "If you've finished your breakfast, get upstairs and clean your room."

I didn't finish my cereal after that. Mom never swears at me. She says swearing is for delinquents with impoverished vocabularies. Mom likes extensive vocabularies—that's why mine is so well developed. She keeps on shoving words down my throat, like omega-3 fish oils. She says it's good

51

for me. Well, I could think of a few choice words to say to her that morning. I went upstairs silently mouthing all the swear words I knew and then I just wanted to cry. That's the first time I had actually wanted to swear at Mom.

I went into her room. I don't know why. I think I was hoping to see some trace of Nice Mom, not the crazy lady who was downstairs cleaning and swearing. And you know what? Her own room was a mess: there were scrunched-up tissues everywhere—on the floor, in the trash, on the floor beside the trash. Her bedside table was the worst—there was a big pile of soggy tissues and four undrunk cups of tea. I sat down on her bed for a minute. It was still warm. I looked at the clock. It wasn't even seven yet. Lots of time.

If I was going to commune with the spirit of Nice Mom, what better place to do it than in her great big cozy bed? I pulled back the covers and there was Sir Fluffington staring up at me with his one eye. He lost the other eye in a battle with next door's psychotic Chihuahua when I was five. Have you ever heard the expression "Time heals all wounds"? Well, take it from me, it doesn't. It has been seven years since the Battle of Wounded Eyeball, and I still regard that dog and his owner (forever after known as Mrs. Chihuahua) as the enemy.

I looked down at Sir Fluffington. Mom must have been feeling nostalgic for the old days too, because she doesn't normally take a teddy bear to bed. I yawned and realized I'd had less than four hours of sleep. And you know what they say, children need a lot of sleep for development. Well,

I didn't want to be underdeveloped, so I got into bed, took one great big sniff of Sir Fluff's head (it smelled of memories) and snuggled down. Within minutes I was fast asleep.

I woke to the sound of Mom yelling at me. "What are you doing in my bed?" she shrieked.

It was like being in a cheap TV remake of the Goldilocks story and I had the starring role, only I wasn't a girl and I didn't have golden locks. Mom was so angry and stupefied that I actually thought she was going to explode. Her face was purple and a vein was pulsing on the side of her forehead, like a worm had found its way in there and was trying desperately to find its way out again. Seriously unattractive. If the Three Bears looked anything like that, it's no wonder Goldilocks threw herself from a top-floor window. I leaped out of bed and ran from the room.

Mom was still cleaning when I left for school. She stopped dusting for half a second and came to the front door. "Where are your glasses?" she said.

"They're broken," I said. So much for the clever web of lies I'd planned.

"They're *what*?" The worm in her forehead started pulsing again.

"They're damn well broken," I said, and felt my face boil.

"Don't you swear at me," she snapped.

"Yeah, well. Don't *you* swear at *me*."

I left her there on the doorstep in a nightie, with a duster in her hand. Her eyes were all bulgy like she'd had no sleep even though she'd been on a mega sleepathon, and her hair was uncombed, so she looked like one of those Gorgon monsters with snakes growing out of its head. I really hope no one saw her.

I usually pick up Ang on the way to school, but I didn't that day. I was too depressed. I trudged off, walking d-e-a-d s-l-o-w. My feet felt like they were made of lead. Can your emotions affect your body mass? I'm sure I weighed twice what I had the night before. I felt so heavy. Then I remembered Harry Hill—he might not have written back yet, but I could easily recall every one of his jokes about wacko, crazy moms. So I did. And that cheered me right up.

It's good to know you're not alone.

11
FATSOANDRATSO

YOU'RE NEVER GOING TO BELIEVE what happened next, but I'm going to tell you anyway.

When I got to school, I dragged Ang down to the girls' locker room because I desperately needed cheering up and I thought a glimpse of The Goddess might just do it. I even put my broken glasses on so I could see her properly. And you know what? I did.

Talking to The Yeti!

He was towering over her and looked even uglier than ever. I nearly lost my mind.

I grabbed Ang's arm. "Look! The Yeti is threatening Lucy. What'll we do?"

"Uh, thank God it's not *you*," Ang said, taking out a chocolate bar.

But I had to do something.

I would go over there and punch that big creep. I would knock him out. I would save Lucy and then maybe she would be really grateful and maybe fall in love with me. Maybe.

"I'm going in," I said.

"No way!" Ang said, choking on his chocolate bar.

"*Way!*"

"Cool!" Ang said. "Can I watch?"

I took a deep breath, pushed my glasses up my nose, and marched up to The Yeti. Then, just as I raised my hand to tap him on the shoulder, Lucy glared at me in horror. Poor Lucy. I'd be horrified too if a creep like that was breathing down my neck.

The Yeti turned and snorted. "Well, if it isn't Fatso and Ratso."

The Goddess giggled nervously.

It was obvious who was Ratso and who was Fatso because I am ultra-thin in an attractive, stick-insect kind of way, and Ang is a tiny bit plump in a non-stick-insect kind of way. This was bad. Really bad. Ang hates it when people comment on his size. I did tell you he was sensitive about it. The thing is, he isn't fat, really, just a bit round and soft, like a Teletubby, but without the television screen for a stomach. And he wasn't about to let a big (and genuinely fat) oaf like The Yeti call him Fatso.

He was going to do something stupid. I could feel it.

I was right. Just as The Yeti was making himself a nice big fist, Ang stepped out from behind me and said, "I have three words for you, Yeti-man: pot, kettle, and black."

"Huh?" The Yeti said, looking to me for explanation.

I looked at Ang. He was about to get his face pulped by two hundred pounds of Yeti and all he was worried about was kitchenware. I scratched my head and that's when I remembered I was wearing my broken glasses. In front of Lucy! We had to get away.

"*What*?" I mouthed desperately to Ang.

"You know," he said, "the pot calling the kettle black. People in glass houses not throwing stones and stuff."

Glass houses? Now he'd moved on to gardening. Isn't fear a strange and powerful thing, the way it can make you lose your mind like that?

The Yeti and I stared at him like he was speaking Japanese.

"Huh?" The Yeti said again.

My Grandpa Joe used to say crazy stuff like this before he died, but he was suffering from dementia, so he had an excuse. He'd been a boxing coach and Mom said that he'd gotten damaged from too many blows to the head.

Hey! That was it! Ang was suffering from brain damage. "Wow!" I said to The Yeti. "You are good. *A-mazing*. You haven't even laid a finger on him and already he's suffering from a concussion."

And—holy saucepan lids!—The Yeti laughed. He opened his great big slimy Yeti mouth and roared. Then he forgot all about pummeling us to death and walked off chortling to himself.

And then—wait for it—The Goddess turned to Ang and me. I figured she was warming up for a sneer because Holly and The Meerkats were watching from the entrance to the girls' locker room. But you know what? I didn't care. I had defused a serious Yeti situation without bloodshed and I was so impressed with myself that I was considering a career in conflict resolution. I think there really is such a job.

Anyway, The Goddess stood before us, swished back her

hair in that excruciatingly exquisite way she has, and said, "We don't think you're fat, Ang—just sort of cuddly." She looked at me. "And I don't think you're a rat," she said. "At least, hardly ever."

Then she swished her hair again and walked off. Ang stared at me. He was smiling. A lot.

"I'm not fat," he said. "I'm *cud-lee*."

"And I am not a rat," I said.

I walked around for the rest of the day feeling twenty pounds lighter than I had that morning. Somebody really should do some research into the relationship between mood and body mass. I was so light and happy that I actually felt like skipping, but I didn't because I'm not a complete lunatic. Still, you have to admit that things were looking up. I couldn't wait to tell Harry Hill.

Dear Harry Hill,
I hope you are well and not sick or seriously
injured. I only say this because I've written
twice now and you still haven't written back.
I thought I'd let you know that I had a breakthrough today. I made a bully laugh. After that,
he left me alone.

Have you noticed how people can't look
really scary when they're laughing? Weird.

Otherwise, my problems haven't gone away—
Mom is still acting weird and I still need help
with the poetry. So I would be really grateful if
you could hurry up and write back as quickly as
possible.

Yours sincerely,
Philip Wright

12
SAINTPHILIP

YOU'D THINK after a day like that, nothing could ruin
my good mood. Well, you'd be wrong.

When I got home from school, I found the front door
open and Susie's car in the driveway. Inside the house there
were boxes all over the place. Mom was bent over one of
them, rummaging through it. She was wearing her nightie
tucked into a pair of old jeans and her hair was in the same
crazy Gorgon mess as it had been that morning. *Plus* she
had no makeup on.

Let me tell you about my mom: she is vain. I mean, if
letting your only beloved son slave away making breakfast
while you put your makeup on and blow-dry your hair
isn't vain, then I don't know what is. Mom never leaves
the house without full makeup and hair. Once, when we'd
slept in and were late, she nearly crashed the car when
she slammed on the brakes and yelled, "Oh my God! I've
forgotten my face!"

She very nearly caused a pileup. But she didn't, so it
was unfair of the driver behind us to get out of his car and
shout at Mom and tell her she was a stupid idiot woman.
She isn't stupid; she's vain.

Anyway, the point is, for Mom to be up and about without her "face" on and sporting crazy hair and PJs in the middle of the afternoon was a sure sign that things were seriously very, *very* bad.

Susie came out of the kitchen carrying a box.

"We're off to the dump," Mom said. "Wanna come?"

"You're in your nightie," I said. "People do not go out in their nightwear unless they're sleepwalking or they've just escaped from a lunatic asylum."

Susie opened her mouth to speak but Mom silenced her with one of her looks.

She turned back to me. "Suit yourself," she said. And they left.

Without me.

I didn't know what to do then, so I wandered aimlessly around the house, which was so clean I hardly recognized it. I felt rotten—I love going to the dump and they'd gone without me—but most of all, being mean to Mom was no fun, even though I was in the right. I resolved to make it up as soon as she got back. And then I saw my room.

It was spotless.

Yes, I will admit that the room needed tidying. Yes, it had gotten really bad. Yes, there may have been a slice or two of pizza moldering under a heap of stinky socks—but that did not give Mom the right to go marauding through my things. I don't suppose marauders tidy up after themselves, but you know what I mean. The whole room was in order: books were on shelves, clothes were in drawers, and my shoes were all neatly lined up in pairs. If a TV detective came into this room he would say a serial killer lived here. TV serial killers are always neat freaks. That's how you can spot them. They're always trying to keep things in order; then they lose control and kill lots of untidy people. I know this because I saw it on *CSI* once.

I looked around my serial killer's room and that's when I saw it: a sheet of paper neatly folded up on my pillow. I recognized the page immediately and felt my stomach lurch.

Mom had read my poem. My *love* poem. To a *girl.*

I was so mad I considered running away, just to teach her a lesson. But I knew that was stupid. I had nowhere to go and no money and no running-away stuff. I didn't even own a sleeping bag. Besides, I like my comforts, you know, like food and a bed.

That got me thinking about all those poor people you see sleeping in shop doorways and begging on the street. Their moms must have been really mean to them to make them choose that life. I resolved there and then that the next time I passed one of those people, I would give them some of Mom's money, and maybe even some of her un-wanted junk. And that's when I had this amazing idea.

I filled two backpacks with Mom's castoffs from the boxes in the hall. There were clothes and books and kitchen things and a whole load of other stuff. There were even some things belonging to Dad, so you can tell how often Mom cleared things out. I found an old jacket of his, some shirts, two ties, and some underpants. I didn't think anyone would want someone else's icky underpants so I left those behind. But I took the ties because I thought they could come in handy for tying up wounds to stop bleeding. You know, the way they do in movies.

I grabbed my keys and wrote Mom a note. "Gone out" was all it said, which was nicely pointless because it would be obvious that I'd gone out, since I wouldn't be in. I left my phone beside the note so she would know she couldn't contact me. I thought that was a clever and hurtful thing to do because I knew she would be worried. Well, tough. I was fed up being the one doing all the worrying around here. It was her turn.

It was just after four when I got into town and I was a bit worried that it was too early to find the homeless people, but then I saw an old man sitting in the doorway of a convenience store.

"Hi," I said cheerfully.

He didn't answer.

It hadn't occurred to me that conversation would be a problem.

I couldn't think of anything to say to him, so I told him a joke. A golden oldie. You can never go wrong with a classic. "What do you get if you cross a chicken with a cement mixer?"

"What?" the man said.

"A bricklayer," I said, and the old man smiled.

I did a little dance around him, then spread my arms out and said, "Ta-daa! I used to be a tap dancer, but I kept falling in the sink."

The man's smile widened. He couldn't help himself. I *am* very funny.

"Um," I said, "would you like a scarf or a hat or maybe a nice book to read?"

The man looked at me like I was insane, but when I started to take stuff out of the bags he realized I was serious. In the end he took a scarf, both ties (he must really live in fear of bleeding to death), Dad's old jacket, and a pair of ski socks. He looked especially pleased with the jacket. I felt good then. Really good. Like a saint or something. I think maybe I'll become a monk or a missionary if the comedy doesn't work out.

"What are you doing?" a girl's voice said.

I turned around and couldn't believe my eyes. It was The Goddess. I was SO glad I'd decided not to wear my broken glasses.

"What are you doing?" she asked again.

"Nothing," I managed to say.

"You're not doing nothing; you gave that old man clothes. I saw you."

"Um, I ..."

"Can I help?" she said.

"I, um ..."

"I'll take that as a yes," she said, taking one of my backpacks and marching off.

The next person we met was a woman selling paper flowers near the post office. She didn't speak much English, so a joke was out of the question, but eventually, with

64

lots of miming and gesturing, she realized what we were there for.

She took one of Dad's shirts, a sweater, a woolly hat, and a baby blanket. The woman gave Lucy one of her paper flowers, which I half expected her to sneer at, because her dad is rich and she can have real flowers any day of the week if she wants them. But she actually looked really happy with it. I liked Lucy for liking the flower. It made her less goddessy.

After that, we met a man with a dog. He looked quite young, about nineteen, maybe (the man, not the dog). I felt a bit creeped out by him. He had a mean look on his face and he made a low noise in his throat that made the dog growl. Neither Lucy nor I moved.

"Never seen a dog before?" he said.

"Of course," I said, trying not to sound scared, then added in a very squeaky voice, "My dog is really badly behaved; he chases everyone on a bike."

"Yeah?" the man said through his mean-looking teeth.

"So I took his bike away," I said, and smiled weakly.

The man bent down to his dog.

"Did you hear that, Pip? The boy's a comedian." When he lifted his head again, he was smiling.

We showed the man what we had left. He took a hand-knitted blanket for Pip to lie on and that book about staying calm from Mom's inner-peace phase.

When we'd left him, Lucy said, "My mom would kill me if she knew what I was doing."

"Where does she think you are now?"

"Swimming," she said, pointing to the swim bag slung over her shoulder.

"Why aren't you?" I asked.

"Du-uh! Because I'm here with you."

I went a bit pink in the face and dived into the backpack. "Let's see what's left."

"I wish I had something to give people," Lucy said. "When I go home I'm going to gather up all the things my family never use, and give them to people. Redistribution of wealth—my dad'll kill me." And she burst out laughing, as though getting killed by her dad was the most fun a person could have.

Being with Lucy was amazing. I could not believe my luck, *and* she had the bright idea to go down by the river, where we met a big group of homeless people. They were all crouched together laughing about something. I hoped it wasn't me, because I hadn't said anything funny yet.

We left them everything—socks, shirts, mittens, a pack of cards, and a salad spinner. One of the men put the salad spinner on his head.

"Why did the tomato blush?" I said.

"Because it saw the salad dressing," the man with the salad spinner hat said.

And we all laughed. All except one girl, who was sitting apart from the group.

"She didn't get anything," Lucy said.

"There's nothing left," I said, holding up the empty backpacks.

Lucy grimaced. Then she took her swimming bag from her shoulder. She pulled out a very fluffy, very pink towel and a tub of some kind of cream that looked like it came from a really fancy shop. She handed the things to the girl.

"Lush," the girl said, opening the tub and taking a sniff.

Lucy turned to me and smiled. The most beautiful smile in the world.

13
BLINDMAN'S BLUFF

I TAKE IT ALL BACK. Love *is* wonderful. I was delirious. And if my body-mass/mood theory was anything to go by, I must have weighed next to nothing. I was very nearly floating.

And I suddenly felt really generous. I wanted everyone to be as happy as I was, especially Mom. So when I got home, I let myself in and went straight to the kitchen to make her a nice cup of tea. Mom loves tea. But before I had even filled the kettle, I overheard Susie talking in the next room.

"You're going to have to tell him sooner or later," she said.

"I know," Mom said, sounding irritated. "Stop pressuring me. He's only twelve, remember."

What did she mean, *only* twelve? I am nearly thirteen.

"Tell me what?" I said, coming into the room (minus the tray of tea I'd planned).

They stared at me in pure horror. I wondered if my fly was undone, but I didn't check because I didn't want to draw attention to my downstairs department.

"You need new glasses," Mom said. "I'll take you tomorrow." Then she turned to Susie. "You see? I can't do this." She sounded really weird, like her voice was cracking in two.

My stomach tightened and I felt a small snake of ice slither down my spine. Was my eyesight that bad? If I was going blind, there wasn't a lot I could do about it. I would just have to be content with some dark glasses and a stick. And maybe even a guide dog. Cool. A Labrador. I hoped it would be black. I prefer black Labradors to the golden ones.

"Tell him," Susie said, interrupting my plans for going blind.

"I can't," Mom said in her horrible crackly voice.

She was so upset, anyone would think *she* was the one going blind.

"You have to," Susie said.

Mom breathed deeply. "I have to go to the hospital," she said.

"What kind of hospital?" I asked. Please, please let it not be a high-security mental hospital.

"A hospital hospital," Mom said, "with sick people and nurses."

"Your mom needs to have an operation," Susie said.

"*Surgery*!" I squawked. "On your head?"

"My head?" Mom said, looking at me like *I* was the crazy one. She put a hand up to her head as if to check it was still there. "No, not my head," she said.

"Where?" I said.

"St. Mary's," Mom said. Susie sighed.

"No, *where*?" I said.

"Umm," Mom said, and looked at Susie.

"Where on your body?" I said.

"Umm, uh," Mom said.

"*WHERE*?"

Mom opened her mouth to speak, but only a squeak came out.

Susie and I took a step closer, egging her on. It was like a scene from a crime movie where you're about to hear whodunit just before the victim croaks.

Mom coughed and closed her eyes. When she opened them again they were all watery. Then she started saying some nonsense words. "I have a t . . . um . . . a gro . . . er . . . umor."

"You have a rumor?" I said. "Is it spreading?"

Nobody laughed. That annoyed me, because, face it: that was funny.

"A tumor," Mom said quickly. "Like a cyst."

Susie sighed again.

Mom glowered at her.

"A cyst?" I said to Mom in my best voice of contempt. I'd had a cyst once (on my finger). No way was it this big a deal.

"A cancer tumor," Mom said. Her voice was this tiny little whisper.

"A *what*?" I choked.

"Don't make me say it again," Mom said, still in her

whispery voice. She sounded like she didn't have enough air to breathe.

"Cancer," Susie said.

"Who asked you?" I snapped.

Susie was around here far too much these days.

I turned to Mom. "You can't have cancer," I said. My voice sounded desperate.

"I know I can't," Mom said in this deadly quiet voice, "but I do."

"But people die of cancer," I said, and I immediately regretted it because both Mom and Susie started crying.

"Not always. Not nowadays," Susie said, recovering. "They can fix it now."

I didn't believe this. "How do they fix it?" I asked.

Mom took off her glasses and mopped her eyes with a tissue.

"Well, first there's the surgery," she said, "then radio–therapy."

Radiotherapy. I imagined Mom lying in a darkened room listening to Classic FM. I saw her with cucumbers on her eyelids and a towel around her head.

"What exactly is radiotherapy?" I asked.

"Radiation therapy," Susie said. "They zap the area with X-rays and . . ."

"*Radiation!*" I yelled. "Are you crazy? Radiation killed Dr. Who in that Christmas special we watched. Don't you remember? Five hundred thousand rads of the stuff, just before David Tennant regenerated into Matt Smith."

"I fell asleep five minutes in," Mom said.

"And after the radiation, then what? Will you be better then?" I asked.

"I'll probably have to have chemotherapy too," Mom said.

"*Kee-mo-therapy!*" I squawked. "What's kee-mo-therapy?"

"Drugs," Susie said. "They inject them into your body and it kills the cancer."

"Cool," I said. "Like chemical warfare."

"Yeah, cool," Mom said, but she didn't really sound like she meant it. "There are side effects," she said. "You can get really tired."

"You're already really tired," I said.

"Well," Mom said, sounding a bit exasperated, "I'll be even more tired. And maybe a bit sick." She turned to Susie. "The nurse told me that one woman puked into her purse because she was on a bus and had nowhere else to spew."

"Ick!" Susie said, then turned to me. "Quick! Hide all the purses."

Suddenly Susie was a comedian. I didn't laugh.

"And," Mom said, "my hair might be affected. Parts of it might fall out."

"What, like *lumps* of it?" I said. "Won't that look a bit weird?"

Mom looked like she was going to cry again.

"Philip, listen to me. My hair will fall out if they give me chemotherapy. All of it."

"All of it?" I said. This was ridiculous.

"Yes, all of it."

"What, even your nose hairs?" I said.

She couldn't seriously mean *all* of it.

"Yes, even my nose hairs," Mom said. The corners of her eyes and mouth drooped.

"That was supposed to be a joke," I said. "Are you serious? Every hair on your body will fall out? You'll be as smooth as an egg?"

"Eggs-actly," Mom said.

I didn't really think her egg joke was funny, but I laughed anyway.

"It'll grow back," Susie said, "and it'll be better than ever."

"When is it happening?"

"On Tuesday," Susie said.

"But that's just days away! You can't. It can't . . ."

Mom didn't speak. Her silence filled the room. It crept into my ears and eyes, into my nose and my throat, and suddenly we were crying. All three of us.

I'm not sure why they were crying, but I was crying because I didn't want a baldy mom. Bald was all right for people like Harry Hill, but not my mom. When we'd stopped crying I realized she still hadn't told me where the cancer was.

"Where is it?" I asked.

Susie opened her mouth to speak. "It's . . ."

"I'm not asking you," I said through my teeth. "I'm asking Mom."

"Breast cancer," Mom said in a very small voice. "It's in my . . ."

"No!" I shouted.

No. No. No. NO! Anything but that. Anything but the B word. How could she do this to me? Now everybody would be saying the word "breast" all the time as if it were some ordinary everyday word like "teapot." Why couldn't she have bowel cancer instead? On second thought, maybe not. I didn't want people imagining Mom on the toilet. Lung cancer, maybe? No, people died of that all the time on TV. What about toe cancer or ear cancer? I could live with that.

Susie broke the silence. "They remove the breast and—"

See what I mean. It would be *breast, breast, breast* from there on in. Hold on, did she say remove it? Cut it off!

"Shut up," I said. "Shut up. Shut up."

"Maybe I should go," Susie said.

"Yeah, maybe you should," I said, which really wasn't like me.

"Philip!" Mom said. "Don't be so rude. I want Susie to stay."

"Suit yourself," I snapped.

I was fed up with this. I didn't want to think about Mom being sick. I wanted to think about Lucy. And about giving stuff to poor people with her. Instead, my head was crammed with images of hospitals with killer X-ray machines and one-boobed, bald-headed women barfing into purses.

"You've ruined everything," I said to Mom. "What am I going to do about Lucy now?"

Mom and Susie stared at each other.

"Who's Lucy?" they said in unison.

74

Dear Harry Hill,

I've been wondering how you went bald. I've always assumed you just shaved your hair off because it looks good for your act, but now I'm not so sure. Did it just fall out with old age or did you take medicine to make it fall out? If it was the medicine, can you please write and tell me what that was like? I've just found out what's wrong with Mom. She's lost her sense of humor because she's going to have to take that medicine too.

No offense, but I think you'll agree that, while it's a good look on you, it's different for women. Can you suggest anything I could do to cheer her up? I know that this is something you can help with because you are bald and funny and you used to be a doctor. Please write back quickly, I'm getting desperate.

Yours sincerely,
Philip Wright

14
THE SILENT TREATMENT

HAVE YOU EVER SULKED FOR AGES?

And ages.

Jeeeez, it's boring. After Mom had dropped her bomb-shell, I'd stomped off to my room to lie on my bed and play games on my cell phone forever. But then the battery went dead and I couldn't recharge it because that would've involved finding the strength to sit up and reach the plug at the bottom of the bed. Sulking is seriously exhausting; that plug seemed very far away. Boy, was I bored! And starving.

Rule number one of sulking: eat first.

I wished Ang was with me; then I wouldn't have been starving. He never leaves the house without a chocolate bar in case of emergencies. He's very worried about dropping dead from sudden acute sugar deficiency. If I ever get stuck in a plane crash miles from anywhere, I want Ang to be there too. He'd have tons of treats to munch on before we'd have to start eating each other's limbs.

The more I thought about Ang and his chocolate-filled pockets, the hungrier I felt. I got up and rummaged through my dresser, hoping to find a half-eaten chocolate bar or a bag of chips, but there was nothing. But I did make one brilliant find: an old pair of glasses that I'd forgotten I still had. I loved those glasses—they had tiny Scooby-Doos on the frames. I'd be able to see again, sort of—the lenses weren't strong enough and they were a bit too small. Well, more than a bit; it felt like a wire coat hanger was clamped to my face, but they'd do for a day or so until Mom took me glasses shopping. That got me thinking: Do people with cancer actually go shopping? I pictured a supermarket full of people in hospital gowns, miserably pushing carts around like zombies in a not very good supermarket-zombie movie.

But I was still hungry. And bored.

If you have any doubt about how bored I was, the next thing I did will convince you: I started thinking about Mrs. Gray's poetry—that "Ode to a Nightingale" one with the sore buttocks, by Keats. And that's when I thought maybe Keats wasn't crazy, just bored like me. Let's face it, you'd have to be pretty bored to end up writing poems to birds. Still, a bird friend was better than nothing.

I got up and opened the window, but all I could see was an ancient teddy-mauling Chihuahua who was sleeping under the big pine tree that separated our yards. No birds.

I had a pair of rolled-up socks in my hand, from rummaging around in the drawers, so I took aim and flung the socks at the dog. Don't ask me why. Just because it was there. Like Everest.

The socks landed on the Chihuahua's head. He woke up and sneezed from the shock, then started attacking the socks with his gums.

I went back and had another rummage for harmless missiles. Revenge had come at last. In the end I decided to stick with rolled-up socks. I didn't want to hurt the mutt, just teach him a lesson, and I only used boring school socks—nobody would miss those.

I'd only been at it for a minute or two when I heard voices outside. Old Mrs. Chihuahua was shouting and Susie was saying something I couldn't make out and the next thing I knew, footsteps were thundering up the stairs.

Mom burst in just as I was preparing to fling a three-in-one sock special out the window.

My face boiled.

"Philip," Mom gasped, "Mrs. Casey says you're attacking her dog. Your socks are all over her lawn."

I was so flustered, I forgot that I wasn't talking to her.

"How do you know they're mine?" I said, which you have to agree was not clever.

I waited for Mom to start bawling me out. She's not generally a shouter but will rise to the challenge when she has to. But you know what? She didn't. She just sat on my bed and said that old Mrs. Chihuahua was downstairs threatening Susie with the police and the ASPCA and social services and Meals on Wheels and the Mega Lottery and God knows what.

"The lottery?" I said.

"*Joke*, Mr. Comedian," Mom said, and kicked off her shoes. Then she settled herself on top of my bed. "Are those your old kiddie glasses?"

I touched my hand to the frames. I didn't like her calling them kiddie glasses. Scooby-Doo appeals to viewers of all ages, doesn't he?

"What were you thinking, you big nitwit?" she said.

"I wasn't."

"Evidently," Mom said, closing her eyes and leaning back on my headboard.

It had been a long time since Mom had sat on my bed like that. She used to do it all the time when I was little, to read to me and tell me stories about when she was a child. I loved that. I stared at Mom, waiting for her to open her eyes and tell me off. I wished she'd hurry up and get it over with, but she just sat there. I thought maybe she was trying out a new tactic designed to prolong the agony and make me squirm. Well, it worked. I was squirming.

After what felt like hours, but was in fact about five minutes, I couldn't take any more. "I'm sorry. I shouldn't have done that to Mrs. Casey's dog," I said in my most repentant voice, and I genuinely meant it. I hate that dog for what he did to Sir Fluffington, but I'd never actually harm him. Not that throwing *socks* at the mutt was going to hurt anything other than his dignity. Mom didn't answer.

"Mom?" I said.

She was taking this silent torture thing a bit too far. I waited another few minutes, then I leaned over her and poked her gently in the ribs, but she didn't even flinch.

"Mom?"

She let out a small snort and her mouth fell open slightly. Fast asleep. Poor old Mom. It must be really exhausting having cancer *and* a crazy, Chihuahua-hating son. She looked lovely lying there, all cozy and sleepy, and not shouting. Her glasses were crooked, so I very carefully slipped them off and put them on my bedside table. She looked even nicer then, softer or something. I pulled a blanket up and tucked it around her shoulders, then went downstairs to face the music.

15
LUNCHHERO

ANG LOVED the whole Chihuahua-sock saga.

"What did old Mrs. Chihuahua do to you?" he asked when I told him the story in the lunch line the following day. I hadn't told him *why* I'd been hurling socks out my window. We're good friends, but I wasn't ready to tell him that my mom would soon be minus one in the boob department.

"She gave me juice and doughnuts with coconut on top," I said.

"Cool," Ang said. "And then did she call the police?" He seemed really eager for me to get arrested.

"No," I said. "She poured me more juice. I think she felt sorry for me."

"Why would she feel sorry for you?"

"Dunno, but she kept on saying, 'You poor dear,' so she must have."

"So," Ang said, scratching his head, "you attack Crazy Dog Woman's pooch with smelly socks and she feeds you doughnuts?"

"They weren't smelly and she's not crazy," I said. "She's actually really nice."

Call me a hypocrite, but I didn't like Ang talking about old Mrs. C like that. And yes, I do know that I was the one who christened her Mrs. Chihuahua, but I still didn't like Ang making fun of her. Not now that she'd given me doughnuts.

But Ang wasn't giving up.

"When I first moved here you made me swear to make Mrs. Casey and her mutt my mortal enemies."

"So?"

"So I could have been drinking juice and eating home-made doughnuts instead. Next you'll be telling me she carries the dog around in her purse and kisses its head, like Paris Hilton and her mutt."

"Um, she does kiss Alfred Pickles quite a lot," I said, squirming. "Wonder what's for lunch today."

"Who the heck is Alfred Pickles and what's he got to do with anything?"

"That's his name—the dog," I said, hoping Ang would drop the subject.

I felt rotten because everything Ang knew about Mrs. Chihuahua and her dog came from me. But if he'd only seen them together, he'd change his mind. Boy, those two are crazy about each other. Mrs. Chihuahua let Alfred Pickles climb up onto her lap and lick her face and slobber all over her. She even took off her slippers and let him lick her feet, which was a bit gross—old people have really ugly feet, all gnarled and knobbly like tree roots. Still, it was kind of nice watching the two of them together. They were like best friends or something. It got me thinking that Mom should get a dog. I mean, I'm not going to be around forever and she'll need something to fill the void when I leave home.

The lunch line moved half an inch forward and then a crowd of eighth-graders came in and cut in front of some terrified-looking sixth-graders and we were back where we started. I expected Ang to start complaining because he gets a bit cranky when he's hungry, but he didn't seem bothered because he just stood there smiling into the distance. I was about to start one of my when-I-rule-the-world speeches (I was planning on life imprisonment for line cutters) when I spotted Lucy and her meerkat friend scanning the crowd for someone.

I craned my neck and stood on my toes. *Here, I'm over here.*

And then, I could not believe my eyes. Right there and then, in full view of everyone, Lucy stopped, took out her purse, and handed over its contents.

To The Yeti.

Ang saw it too, but oddly he just kept on smiling like a simpleton.

The Yeti smirked at Lucy and landed his big fat ugly hand on her shoulder. That was it. I clenched my fist and stepped out of the line. The Yeti was in for it this time.

Ang pulled me back. "You do know you're wearing Scooby-Doo glasses, don't you?" he said.

"That big creep is bullying Lucy for her lunch money. She must be terrified."

"She doesn't look terrified," Ang said, and I felt like punching him too.

Of *course* Lucy was scared.

I went after her. And you know what? Ang came too. He actually left a line for food and went with me to save Lucy. What a friend!

As soon as we were face-to-face, Lucy went all goddessy, giggling and mumbling something to her friend about Scooby-Doo, and at that very same moment something happened to the wiring in my brain: eighty percent of my neurotransmitters must have shut down because instead of saying, "Lucy, are you all right?" only grunts and mangled bits of words came out.

I took off my Scooby-Doo glasses because I was feeling self-conscious, but then I couldn't see properly and I was squinting at Lucy like a weirdo. Weirdo squinting stalker is not a good look on me, so I put the glasses back on.

"Money . . . um. Yeti . . . um . . . lunch . . . um," I said, which in my head translated to, "Lucy, did The Yeti take your lunch money?" but outside my head the words sounded like the chorus of a bizarre and creepy nursery rhyme: "Money-yum, Yeti-yum, lunch-yum."

"Smooth-yum," Ang said, and then he coughed this really noisy cough.

Lucy's friend turned to him. She put a hand on his shoulder and said, "Are you all right? Here, have a sip of my water." Ang coughed again and took the water bottle she held out to him. He was grinning from ear to ear. Idiot. What was there to grin about?

"Did you want something?" Lucy said.

I stared at her and waited for something that sounded like English to come out of my mouth. "Yeti . . . Was he . . . are you . . . did he?" I said, which I think you'll agree was about as clear as mud.

"Are you sick or something?" Lucy said.

"Maybe it's code or a rap or something," the annoying friend said.

And you know what? Ang burst out laughing as if this was the funniest thing he'd ever heard in his entire life.

I shot him a you're-supposed-to-be-my-friend look, but he went on laughing like a hyena. A really stupid hyena that laughs in all the wrong places.

"Did Eddie Lyttle take your money?" I finally managed to say.

Lucy blushed.

She looked down at her feet and her hair fell down over her face. I wanted to reach out and push it back so much. But then she whipped back her hair and snapped at me, "Is that any of your business, Philip Wright?"

That's when I knew I was doomed: girls only call you by your full name when they're truly disgusted with you. And I was right. Lucy told me to stick my nose somewhere it belonged, grabbed her friend's arm, and stomped off.

Holly, the annoying friend, kept looking back over her shoulder. I think she wanted her water bottle back. But Ang was holding it like it was some kind of prize and he was grinning like a goon. I could have punched him.

Dear Harry Hill,

I know you are a busy man, but I am beginning to lose patience with you. I have now written to you four times and you haven't written back once.

Things have gotten a whole lot worse here. Not only do I have Mom to deal with, but I think my bully is now bullying my girlfriend (who isn't really my girlfriend), and my friend Ang (who really is my friend) has started acting weird and has lost interest in his food.

Can't you see what a terrible mess my life is? Don't you feel anything when a fellow comedian is suffering? Write back soon. Please.

Yours sincerely,
Philip Wright

16
THINKPOSITIVE

PLEASE DON'T GET the wrong impression when I say that I enjoyed Mom going to the hospital. I know I was supposed to be all freaked out about her operation, but the fact is I like hospitals. I can see why Harry Hill was a doctor before he became a comedian. For a start, there's all that saving-people's-lives business, and then there's all the cool equipment they have, like drips and monitors and those paddle things they use to shock people back to life.

The truth is, Mom going to the hospital was kind of exciting, and I think she thought it was exciting too because she was buzzing the day before the operation. When I came home from school, she was furiously cleaning the house again. She was "putting things in order," she said. Anybody would've thought they were going to perform her surgery on the kitchen table, the way she kept scrubbing at it. Since being diagnosed with cancer Mom had become a complete clean freak. She was cleaning the house like her life depended on it, like she was trying to control all the germs in the world and tell them where to go. I could have told her she was wasting her time because cancer isn't caused by germs; it's caused by out-of-control cell growth. I know this because I read it on the internet, but I didn't tell Mom because I didn't want to burst her bubble. I just followed her around and told her a bunch of old jokes to keep her company while she cleaned.

And then (I do feel a tiny bit guilty about this) on the actual day of the operation Susie let me stay home from school *and* she said we could go shopping for new glasses—and I can't pretend I wasn't happy about the school part because I'm only human.

Susie said we should make a day of it, have lunch out and everything. I didn't see how buying glasses could take a whole day, but I went along with it anyway. I was right, I found the pair of frames I wanted right away. But Susie said no. She said Mom would have two hernias and rip her stitches open if we didn't come back with something *sensible*. I think what she really meant was boring. Instead of taking the glasses I wanted (big black frames like Harry Hill's) we spent so much time in the optician's that I was beginning to think blind people had it easy. They didn't have to go through all that business: put on the gray ones; take them off; put on the silver ones; take them off; no, no, put them on again; no, put the gray ones back on; no, not *those* gray ones, *those ones*. After about an hour of that, I felt like gouging my own eyes out with a rusty spoon and saving us all a whole lot of trouble.

Did I tell you that I hate shopping? And after three hours in a shop with me, so did Susie.

"Never again," she said, flopping down into a seat in the café next to the optician's.

I don't think Susie genuinely hated being out with me, it was just that she was really worried about Mom. She kept biting her nails and saying stuff like, "She'll have had her pre-med by now." "She'll be in recovery now." "She'll ..."

Honestly, adults are impossible. Someone should tell them that it's not a good tactic to keep talking about what's worrying you. It only makes matters worse.

And the thing is I wasn't really worried. Mom had told me that everything was going to be all right and I believed her. Mom is *the* person in my life, the one who is just always there, doing stuff, getting on my nerves, knowing everything. I literally couldn't begin to think of anything bad happening to her. When I tried, my mind just went blank like a broken computer screen.

And if you really want to know the truth, I was more worried about Mrs. Gray's poetry session, which was scheduled for the very next day. Why did I ever tell her I was a poet? I am so not poet material. Poets are all tragic and sad and die at an early age. I am comic and happy and plan to live way into my nineties. Not to mention the minor detail that I can't actually write poetry. And I had to come up with Volume 1 for my personal poetry session in less than twenty-four hours.

You know how you hear writers on TV talking about writing? I say writers, but I've only ever heard one, on a kids' show. Well, he said you should write about yourself or something you know. Generally, I think that is terrible advice because most people just know about getting up and going to school or work, then coming home and having their dinner. Who wants to read about that? I like reading adventure/crime/action/sci-fi novels and I don't for one minute believe my favorite writers have garroted a Russian spy with cheese wire, hung upside down from a flagpole over a busy London street, or traveled to Mars. So I'm taking that piece of advice with a pinch of salt. However, it did get me thinking about myself and my predicament, or rather Mom's, and I had this brilliant idea that maybe I could write a poem about that.

Oh boob, goodbye
Oh boob, farewell,
Oh mother, do not cry,
With that big woolly jacket on,
No one could ever tell.

On second thought, maybe not.

"Are you any good at writing poems?" I asked Susie.

"What? Poems?" she said, gnawing away at her finger-nails. She took her hand out of her mouth. "Do you think we could go and see her?"

"Are you crazy?" I said. "I've only got one poem written so far."

"What?" Susie said, and went on gnawing her fist.

"Oh, *Mom*, of course," I said, trying to push all thoughts of poetry out of my head. "They told us we can't visit her

90

until after three, remember?"

"I know, but ..." Susie said, chewing her nails some more. Her self-cannibalism was starting to freak me out, so I decided to distract her with a joke.

Patient: Doctor, doctor, every time I drink a cup of tea
          I get a stabbing pain in my eye.
Doctor: Try taking the spoon out first.

It worked! Susie laughed so much she nearly swallowed her own fist.

"You are a tonic, Philip," she said. "With you around your mom can't go wrong. You know, they say your chances of getting better increase if you're positive and cheerful. It's called PMA, Positive Mental Attitude."

"You mean jokes are actually medically good for you? Cool!"

Maybe I could visit sick people and see if they got better after my performances. Wow! Think about it: I could become a world-famous healing comedian who helps sick people attain health and long life. A bit like Jesus, but with a sense of humor.

I was seriously excited about this whole PMA thing and I decided to write to Harry Hill about it. I agonized about whether or not to apologize for telling him I was mad at him in my last letter, but in the end I decided not to. I might end up making matters worse. I couldn't risk upsetting Harry Hill. With Mom sick, I needed him more than ever.

Dear Harry Hill,

Have you heard of PMA? It stands for Positive Mental Attitude. It is amazing; apparently, sick people can make themselves better if they stay positive and happy. I know it sounds a bit far-fetched, but I thought you might know some-thing about it. And if you don't, I could look into it for you.

I will make sure I keep Mom positive and happy and see what effect it has on her health, and then I'll let you know what happens. Deal?

Yours sincerely,
Philip Wright

PS: If this PMA thing is true, think of the possi-bilities. It could be the medical breakthrough of the century. We could become famous and rich and Mom would be cured.

(It occurred to me that Harry Hill was already famous and rich, but I left that bit in anyway.)

17
HOMECOMING

I DIDN'T SHOW MOM my new glasses for a few days because I was a bit nervous that she would freak out and shout and injure herself when she saw that they were Harry Hill glasses. But you know what? When I finally walked in wearing them she just said, "Oh no, *you've been framed*," which was quite clever for a sick person, don't you think?

"Don't worry," Susie said. "It was buy-one-get-one-free, so he does have sensible ones too. But for now the look is geek chic!"

"Geek freak," Mom said. And the two of them had a good giggle. I had made Mom laugh and I hadn't even said a word. If there really was anything in this PMA lark, Mom would be cured in no time.

Then a doctor came and spoiled it all.

He told Mom she could go home the following day, and you know what she did? She burst into tears. It just goes to show you can't trust an adult. There she was saying how much she hated the hospital and complaining about how boring it was and how it *smelled*, and how she wanted to be home with me, but all the time she was secretly glad to be there. Like I said, I could see the attraction of the hospital, but one week was enough. It was time for Mom to come home. And I can tell you, I was not impressed to hear she didn't feel the same.

Not only did she not want to be home with me, but she preferred the company of snoring, groaning (her words) strangers. I just couldn't understand it. And what was the doctor going to think of me? He'd probably think I was some kind of hoodlum that Mom was trying to escape. You know, like the kind you see on TV shockumentaries: "I had my vital organs removed to get away from my delinquent son."

I could see the doctor wasn't impressed with either of us, because he didn't let Mom stay. She kept on sobbing that she wasn't ready and that she couldn't cope, but he just looked at her like she was speaking ancient Greek. It really was an impressive display of heartlessness. I felt a bit in awe of him. And it served Mom right for not wanting to come back to me.

She came home the next day, and there followed the worst few weeks of my life. Mom was impossible. She slept a lot and cried a lot and drank a lot of tea. Once when I brought her a cup of tea (in her favorite cup) she said it was the wrong color and burst into tears. Having your boob chopped off must make you color-blind because there was nothing wrong with the color of that tea. And there was nothing wrong with the taste of it either. I know because I took a sip of it to check it was just right before I brought it to her. Just goes to show the thanks you get.

I felt like crying over that tea myself, but I'm not that

94

childish, and anyway I didn't have time. I had a million things to do, like putting in the laundry and taking out the laundry and hanging up the laundry, then taking it down again and folding it and putting it away. I didn't have to do the ironing because Mom thinks me and a hot iron are a dangerous combination. What an insult, but I didn't argue—I was doing plenty as it was. Honestly, all that laundry was enough to make you want to wear the same pair of socks for a week. We could all be a lot more economical with our clothes-wearing. It just isn't worth it.

Eventually, Mom did get up and about and started doing things around the house, but she didn't return to her fanatical pre-operation cleaning frenzy. In fact, the house started to look like a bit of a mess. Obviously, things being in order didn't matter anymore.

Dear Harry Hill,

I'm sorry for saying I was losing patience with you. I know how busy and exhausted you must be watching TV all day, so I'm really sorry. Anyway, you won't have to put up with me for much longer.

Mom has had an operation, sort of like an amputation but I don't want to say what part they chopped off. Anyway, she needs me to do a million things for her, so assuming I don't die of exhaustion, I won't have time to write for a while.

And if I do find any time for writing, I'll be frantically scribbling poems because my English teacher is still waiting to hear my poetry. So if you don't hear from me, it's just because I'm busy or have stabbed myself with my own poetry-hating pen and not because of any bad feeling.

Please forgive me. I am still your number one fan.

Philip Wright

18
THE MIDAS TOUCH—*NOT*

AFTER A FEW WEEKS of lolling around doing nothing
and getting cups of tea brought to her, Mom went back
to the hospital for the next stage. Instead of making Mom
better, the doctors actually made her sicker. They call it
"treatment," apparently.

Poor Mom. When she wasn't sleeping, she was vomiting, and when she wasn't sleeping or vomiting, she was
crying and worrying and demanding cups of tea and then
not drinking them. She kept apologizing for not being fun
anymore, which was very thoughtful of her.

To begin with I just said, "Don't be silly, Mom, you're
sick; no one expects you to be fun." But as time wore on, I
got a bit fed up with it and I did wonder if maybe she could
make a tiny bit more effort to jazz herself up.

And as if all that wasn't enough, the bad things weren't
confined to Mom being sick. Cancer was a cancer on my
life. (I think that's a metaphor.) Everything I tried my hand
at turned to disaster. I was like that King Midas with the
weird curse where everything he touched turned to gold,
except that the things I touched didn't turn to gold; they
turned to a big heap of stinking garbage. Did you know

that if you rearrange the letters of Midas they spell "I'm sad"? Freak-ee or what! Because, believe me, I was sad. And I know you'll agree that I had good cause to be when you hear my long list of bad things. Be warned: this involves the word "breast."

Bad thing number ONE: I said the word "breast" to Mrs. Gray, the English teacher.

Bad thing number TWO: I think Ang is in love with Lucy.

Bad thing number THREE: I think Lucy is in love with Ang.

Bad thing number FOUR: All of Mom's hair fell out.

And that list doesn't even mention the poetry problem. Mrs. Gray kept on at me for weeks about it, and that's how Bad Thing Number One came about.

I'd managed to give Mrs. Gray's poetry session the slip several times by getting myself lunchtime detentions for coughing in health class. Miss Box, the health teacher—that really is her name—dislikes coughing. She dislikes noises of any kind and prefers us to work in complete silence. I think she has some kind of noise-induced persecution complex because she thinks we're always out to trick her and make fun of her. Actually, come to think of it, we are, but only because we'll die of boredom otherwise. Anyway, I did start deliberately annoying Miss Box because she loves lunch-time detentions and that meant I could escape the one-on-one lunchtime English treat that was lined up for me.

But Mrs. Gray caught up with me in the end.

She nabbed me one day as I was trying to scuttle out of her classroom at Friday home time. "Philip Wright," she said, "you've let me down. I waited for you at lunchtime three Wednesdays in a row and you didn't show."

Is red the color of guilt? If so, my ears were as guilty as hell. They were on fire.

"You didn't even bother to explain why," Mrs. Gray went on.

Ang once told me that when you are in trouble you should say nothing, and since I had nothing to say for myself I decided to take his advice. But it only seemed to rattle Mrs. Gray more. She stared at me and waited for me to respond. When I didn't, she said, "I'm very disappointed in you, Philip."

Aww, now why did she have to go and say that? I hate disappointing people. I hate them thinking I'm a no-good lousy louse. Even when I am. I hated disappointing her so much that I opened my mouth right there and then and said, "Why don't we do it now?"

You know how people say "the silence was deafening" and you think that's stupid because silence isn't deafening, it's silent? Well, when you've sat across the table from your English teacher *not* discussing poetry, you'll know what they mean. Mrs. Gray bombarded me with a ton of questions about Wordsworth and the other poets and I just sat there deafening her with my silence. A silence so pure you could hear the molecules in the air move. They made a kind of thumping noise in my head, like a pulse.

It got louder with every second that passed.

"Did the subject matter interest you?" Mrs. Gray probed. I stared at the table. Fascinating things, tables. Most people don't take the time to fully appreciate the table. And I don't just mean its construction and design; if you look closely at its surface you can see tiny scratches and pockmarks and stains. There was even a burn mark on this table where Pete "Gingernut" McKenna had tried to set fire to our test papers last year. He got suspended and we had to take the test again so it was a lose–lose outcome for everyone, but at least you could say there was history in that table.

Mrs. Gray coughed. "Philip? What about your own poetry, then, since mine didn't do it for you?"

And you know what? I was actually relieved. At least I knew what *my* Lucy poem was about. I took a crumpled page from my pocket and set it on top of Pete McKenna's scorch mark.

Oddly, Mrs. Gray didn't seem that impressed with it. A small crease appeared in her forehead as she read; then she folded the page over and said, "Any more?"

"Not quite," I said, which I thought sounded open-ended enough to keep her happy, but I was wrong—the look of disappointment on her face would have broken a monster. "But I'm working on a new one," I said, trying to un-disappoint her.

"Oh?" she said, brightening a bit. "Let's have it."

I stared at her. I stared at the table. I stared at the floor. Mrs. Gray tried to help me along with an encouraging smile. It was more like the kind of smile you'd give a toddler than an almost-teenager, kind of like the aren't-you-a-cute-puppy smiles Ang's mom gives me. Hey! That was it! Thank you, Ang's mom.

I opened my mouth and said in this really dramatic voice, "Where there is love, there is pain."

Mrs. Gray looked impressed. She smiled at me and nodded. I closed my eyes and pressed my fingers to my temples and massaged the skin there to try and make it look like I was being really creative and thoughtful. "Where there is light, there is dark," I said. "Where there is silence, there is noise."

I was impressed. This poetry lark was a breeze; all you had to do was throw some random words together and make sure they all bounced along nicely. I was feeling quite pleased with myself and opened my mouth ready to let my poetic genius pour forth.

"Where there is . . . "

I stalled.

I started again. "Where there is . . . "

I stalled again.

I sat there opening and closing my mouth, but no sound came out.

I was like a goldfish drowning out of water. And yes, I do know what that looks like because in kindergarten Jimmy Palmer took the class goldfish out of its tank so that it could play with us in the sand pit. It didn't like playing in the sand. It died. But not before it had opened and closed its mouth at us, silently crying out for help.

I was that fish.

You know how they say a drowning man's life flashes before him? Well, that's what happened to me. Except it was worse for me because presumably the drowning man didn't have his English teacher breathing down his neck. Well, all the things that had been worrying me crowded into my brain at once: The Yeti, Mom, Harry Hill, Mom, The Goddess, Mom, Ang, Mom, poor people, Mom, chihuahuas, Mom. Can you see a pattern beginning to emerge here? It doesn't take a genius to figure out that I was more worried about Mom than I'd realized. Or maybe it does. Maybe I could be a genius psychologist when I grow up and tell people what's worrying them.

"Philip, are you all right?" Mrs. Gray said.

That's when I realized there were tears starting at the corners of my eyes.

OH MY GOD. STOP. CANNOT CRY IN FRONT OF TEACHER.

"Philip?" she said again in this weird and velvety voice that sounded like a real person, not a teacher. "Would you like to talk about it?"

"Mom," I squeaked and blinked away my tears.

"Ahh," Mrs. Gray said.

"Sick," I squeaked.

"Mmm," she said soothingly.

"Breast," I whispered.

"Hmm?" she said.

"Breast," I said a bit louder. I couldn't get the "cancer"

bit out; it seemed to have lodged at the back of my throat. I tried again.

"Breast," I squawked.

And that was the end of Velvety Voice. Mrs. Gray's face was the color of boiled beets. She shot up out of her chair and backed away from me, buttoning her blouse up to the neck.

Oh my God! Did she think I meant *her* breast?

OH. MY. GOD. Beam me up. NOW!

19
SECRETSANDLIES

I RAN OUT OF SCHOOL and all the way home. I
couldn't wait to tell Ang the whole thing. We hadn't exactly
been seeing eye to eye recently and Mrs. Gray's boobs could
be just the thing to bring us back together.

Part of the problem was that I was being so secretive.
I still hadn't said anything to him about Mom. How could I:
"Hey, Ang. You know my mom's breasts? Well, she's only
got one." What if he laughed? Or worse, what if he went all
quiet and doom-struck?

One of the problems with being secretive is that it's
contagious. Ever since I'd started holding back from Ang,
he'd started holding back from me. He said I was acting
weird but really I think it was him. When I came by, he
said he was busy—Facebooking somebody. What kind of
friend does that? I was his friend with my face right there
on his doorstep; he didn't need some nobody from cyber-
space. And nearly every time I phoned him it went straight
to voicemail. Why would he spend all that time talking to
someone who wasn't me? I know I wasn't my usual fun-
loving self, and OK, I do admit that sometimes I avoided
him in case the conversation came around to Mom, but still.

Some days I couldn't even find him at lunch break. Normally we just meet up. It's not an arrangement or anything, it just kind of happens, but last week he wasn't in his usual spot by the vending machines. (His sweet tooth extends to all and any soft drinks.) Twice I've had to go and track him down. Today I spotted him heading into the library. I thought maybe he was sick, because who goes to the library at lunchtime? So I followed him. I will never forget what I saw: Ang was sitting there like some kind of prince, all cozied up with Lucy and her friend Holly the Meerkat.

They were poring over books and whispering to each other. Lucy's head was so close to his, and their hands were almost touching, and The Meerkat was giggling away like an idiot. It was enough to make a grown boy cry.

I tried to stay angry at Ang but even though he was a low-down, love-rat creep, he was still my friend and I couldn't imagine not hanging out with him. Anyway, I'd given him the cold shoulder all afternoon so I figured he'd been punished enough. I made up my mind to find him, tell him about Mom, and reduce him to a quivering wreck of laughter with my Mrs. Gray's boobs story. And I wouldn't wait; I'd do it right there and then.

But before I got to his house, I saw him step out his front door. He'd changed out of his school clothes and was wearing enough hair gel to wallpaper a room. He waved to someone on the other side of the street, then crossed over to meet them.

The other person was waving back. And smiling. It was Lucy.

I stood there speechless. Lucy's annoying friend Holly the Meerkat was there too. She was waving and giggling and generally being her usual annoying self. They were all so wrapped up in each other they didn't even see me. They just turned and walked away together. All three of them.

Naturally, I followed them. What else could I do?

I tailed them at a safe distance. There could always be some perfectly innocent explanation for all of this. Maybe Lucy was helping Ang with his homework. The trouble was, there were no backpacks, but there was lots of giggling coming from the girls, and Ang was grinning like a chimpanzee with lockjaw. I followed them to the park and when they stopped at the swings I had to duck behind a tree so they wouldn't spot me.

Then I saw a fourth person coming to join them. Lucy waved and beckoned him over. It was Hoodie Guy. What was going on? Was Lucy two-timing Ang with that hoodie creep? Serves him right if she was. He knew I loved Lucy. Hoodie Guy moved in really close to Lucy and said something. Then he turned to Holly and said something that must have been hil-*arious* because they all burst out laughing and she started poking him in the ribs with her stupid fingers. And before you could say "What are you doing, you pack of low-down treacherous traitors?" they were all horsing around and Holly reached up and pulled the guy's hood down and he . . .

Oh my God! It was The Yeti.

I felt like I had been stabbed in the heart. How could Lucy? How could Ang? I noticed a warm, wet feeling on my leg and wondered if my metaphorical stab wound had somehow started bleeding out my shins. I've always liked the idea of being a medical freak, but right then was not the time. Still, I was a bit disappointed when I looked down and didn't see actual bloodstains. I saw dog pee. A nice fresh torrent of the stuff with steam coming off. Alfred Pickles was looking up at me with his great big Chihuahua eyes and peeing on my leg as if it was the most natural thing in the world.

He was out for a walk with old Mrs. Chihuahua and she'd let him off his leash to "go pee-pees" and then she'd lost track of him.

"Alfred," she called. "Pickly-Wickly, where are you?"

I tried to shoo the dog away from me. The last thing a spy needs is a batty old lady and an incontinent dog giving the game away. By the time Mrs. Casey found us, Pickly-Wickly had emptied the entire contents of his bladder onto my leg. Then he decided he wanted the contents back. He grabbed hold of my pant leg and was shaking his head frantically from side to side and growling and backing away from me, all at the same time.

Can dogs be mentally unstable? If so, Alfred "Pickly-Wickly" Pickles was definitely nuts.

"Naughty, naughty," Mrs. Casey crooned, stooping to pick up the dog.

You'd think a tiny old woman like Mrs. Casey would have a tiny old woman voice, wouldn't you? Well, you'd be wrong. She was crowing away at the top of her lungs. How was I going to spy on Ang with her making all that racket?

James Bond never had this problem. I bent down to try and shut her up and help get her lunatic dog off me—Alfred Pickles had seriously strong jaws for a geriatric pooch. When we finally freed my pant leg from his mouth, I stood up to see four faces staring at me.

Yes, you've guessed it: Lucy, Ang, Holly, and The Yeti.

"Have you wet yourself?" The Yeti asked.

"Yeah, because I pee out my kneecaps," I said, trying to sound cool and condescending, but I'm pretty sure my boiled red face was a dead giveaway that I was squirming.

"Your kneecaps?" The Yeti said, as if he actually believed that could happen.

Ang let out a laugh, but he shut up when Holly the Meerkat shoved her elbow into him.

"Don't listen to him, Eddie," The Goddess said. "He thinks he's funny."

"Yeah, you're right, Luce," The Yeti said, turning away. *Luce!*

"Such a naughty boy!" Mrs. Casey said, smothering the dog with her face.

Now, I don't care what anybody says. It was obvious that Mrs. Casey was talking to Pickly flippin' Wickly and not me. Any idiot could have seen that. But you know what they all did—yeah, that's right. They all fell over laughing. Ang most of all—he kept trying to catch my eye, like we were friends or something. Like this was actually funny.

"We're going to be late," Holly the Meerkat said.

"We're going down to the—" Ang started, but Lucy cut him off.

"Philip can't come—he'll smell like dog pee!"

Then Mrs. Casey said, "We need to be getting home, mister. It's way past your bedtime." And they all fell over laughing again.

OK, I am going to say this one more time—she was talking to the dog, do you hear me, *THE DOG*!

As the others started to leave, Ang turned to me. He looked like he was going to say something, but then that seriously annoying meerkat Holly nudged him and he just shrugged and moved off. Traitor.

20
ASS

I'M NOT GOING TO LIE TO YOU; what Ang did really hurt. I stopped speaking to him after that and even though he came up to me a few times at school I just blanked him. Even when he tried to get around me with a joke.

One day he had the nerve to walk right up to me and ask, "How does the man in the moon cut his hair?" And you know what I did? I just turned and walked away, as if Ang was invisible. I didn't even bat an eyelid, not even when he shouted after me, "E-clipse it."

It was really satisfying ignoring Ang like that. For about half a minute. Then it was just lonely and miserable. When Mom first started acting weird I looked forward to school as a refuge, but then Ang and Lucy and The Yeti started acting weird and school was an extra little slice of hell. And we were actually expected to do some work, you know. Teachers kept telling me my work was slipping or that I wasn't trying. They kept overusing the word "potential." Apparently I have it. You tell me—how is a boy with potential supposed to work when his whole life is in a downward spiral of downwardness?

Everything was bad. Friends were bad, school was bad,

and home was bad. It was unbearable. It can't be good for
you to be in a constant state of misery like that. In fact, I
can prove it's not good for you because I developed a new
condition: Accumulated Stress Syndrome. I diagnosed myself because Mom didn't have time to take me to the doctor.
And anyway, I didn't want to burden her. Accumulated
Stress Syndrome—ASS to you and me—occurs when stress
keeps building up day by day until you feel you can't take
the weight of it anymore and your skin erupts in a hideous
rash of acne as if to say, enough is enough.

But the stress just kept coming—Mom's weirdness
had reached new heights. The other day she yelled at me
because I put a spoon in the fork section of the cutlery
drawer (I am not making this up), and then when I said,
"So what?" she took the spoon out and threw it at me!
Seriously, she threw it right at me. It missed, but that's not
the point: Mom had finally gone completely off her rocker.
And then you know what she did? She started bawling her
eyes out, which was seriously unfair because I should have
been the one crying, not her. Luckily, Susie was there at the
time to referee. She says Mom's weirdness is due to a combination of stress and medication, but I think that is just
plain dumb. You'd think being stressed-out about cancer
would make you appreciate life more, make you love people
(me) more, not go around shrieking and hurling spoons
everywhere.

Shortly after the spoon incident, Ang came to the house.
I opened the door and stared at him. I felt like saying,
"Come right on in, you stinking, cheating love rat. Bring

your new girlfriend, Lucy, bring your new best friend, Yeti-man. Come and see my marvelous life with my falling grades and my unrequited love and my one-boobed mother who throws cutlery at me."

Instead I said, "What do you want?"

"Nothin'," Ang said.

"Okay," I said and closed the door.

Half an hour later he texted me and asked me what I was doing. I deleted the text.

Dear Harry Hill,
I know you're not interested in medicine any-more, but would you happen to know any cures for acne? My face is so spotty and lumpy, the geography teacher could use it as a 3-D relief map of the Rocky Mountains. It's my ASS caus-ing it.

Yours sincerely,
Philip Wright

PS: I want my friend Ang back. Any ideas?

21
PILLOW TALK

IT WAS TEN O'CLOCK on a Sunday morning when it happened. I remember the time exactly because I could hear the radio from Mom's bedroom. The ten o'clock news bulletin had just ended when I heard a scream. I stood outside her door for a moment, terrified. I hoped I hadn't made a mistake when I was putting the laundry away the previous day. One stray sock in her underwear drawer was enough to push her over the edge these days. I heard a choking sound and decided there was no option: I would have to go in.

I found Mom staring at her pillow with a stricken face. I stared at the pillow too because I thought, *Oh, here we go, now Mom has developed a fear of messy pillows*, but then I saw it—a small furry animal lying on her pillow, only it wasn't a small furry animal, it was Mom's hair lying there, without her. Mom was holding on to her head with both hands as if she was trying to stop the rest of her hair from falling out, which was really very silly and very sad at the same time.

She didn't speak to me and I didn't speak to her. I just stood beside her and put my hand on her arm and began slowly stroking it. We stayed like that for ages. I honestly have no idea who I was comforting, her or me. Both, I suppose.

Then I walked over to the phone and dialed Susie's number. I didn't tell her what the problem was, but she knew from the sound of my voice that it was something big. How do you tell someone over the phone that your mom is going bald? Impossible. Impossible and ridiculous and insane and cruel and damn well unfair. Yes, damn. Damn damn damn. I don't care who hears me swear now. This was so damn not fair.

Susie came over right away. I think she'd guessed what the problem was because she was already crying when I opened the door. When I brought her upstairs, Mom was still standing there staring at the pillow. Susie asked me if I wanted to go over to Ang's house, but Mom said softly, "No, let him stay."

You have no idea how good that made me feel. Mom had been so irritable with me all the time. I'd heard Susie say that stress can make you sick and I felt *so* guilty. I was always stressing Mom out—getting detentions, breaking my glasses, messing up the cutlery drawer. Sometimes I felt like the cancer was all my fault.

Mom seemed to know what I was thinking. She gave me a hug.

Then Susie said, "Ready?"

Mom nodded and I stepped back to let them through the door and watched as they locked themselves in the bathroom.

I had no idea what to do then, so I just sat down at the top of the stairs outside the bathroom and waited. I heard a buzzing sound coming from the room and I thought, *I will never understand women.* All they could think to do at a time like that was brush their teeth. Together. (You have got to admit that that is weird.)

When they didn't stop after the two minutes of cleaning Mom always insists upon I called out, "What's with the marathon toothbrushing session?"

But they just ignored me and went on brushing for ages. And ages. While I waited outside on tenterhooks. I have no idea what tenterhooks are, but anyway, I've heard the word used in that kind of way many times and I like the sound of it, don't you? I'll look it up sometime when this is all over.

It turned out that the sound I heard wasn't an electric toothbrush duet; it was Mom's electric leg razor. Susie had used it to shave off what was left of Mom's hair. She came out of the bathroom and poked a finger behind her glasses to wipe away a stray tear. I told her she didn't look too bad, but honestly, she looked awful. She smiled nervously at me and I smiled back, hoping she couldn't tell what I was thinking.

Then Susie said we all deserved a big Sunday breakfast and led Mom down the stairs. When they'd gone, I went into the bathroom and locked the door. It was my turn for a cry.

Dear Harry Hill,
I hope I'm not distracting you from getting ready for your new (can't wait) TV series; ironing those enormous shirt collars must be really time-consuming. But I just had to write.

It has finally happened. And it is every bit as bad as Mom said it would be. The chemotherapy drugs have made all Mom's hair fall out and she doesn't look like Mom anymore. She looks like you. I didn't want to tell you the details of her illness, but I suppose the chemotherapy is a bit of a giveaway. So now you know.

Yours sincerely,
Philip Wright

PS: I'm beginning to think PMA isn't all it's cracked up to be, so don't make any firm plans yet about a career in health-care entertainment.

22
DESPERATEMEASURES

MOM STOPPED GOING OUT. I'm serious—she stayed in the house all day, every day and, as far as I could tell, did absolutely nothing. *Nothing.* The house would be a mess when I'd get back from school and the curtains would still be closed and you can bet your life savings that if she'd still had hair, it would definitely not have been combed.

Sometimes she would be back in bed with a mess of cups and plates and tissues around her. She even started shopping online just so she wouldn't have to leave the house. The only time she went out was to attend one of her hospital appointments and then she wrapped herself up in so many layers (wig and scarf and hat) you'd have trouble identifying her in a lineup. I think that was the point.

But it was pointless because you could tell something was up. Even old Mrs. Chihuahua noticed, and I think she's half blind. She very kindly started bringing over thermoses of old-lady soup, which was surprisingly yummy and didn't taste like boiled knitting, as you might expect. I tried to get Mom to answer the door and take the thermoses from Mrs. C, but she wouldn't budge.

I was beginning to fear that Mom was turning into one

of those crazies you hear about who don't leave the house for decades and who collect used bottle caps and empty chip packages for a hobby. (I saw a documentary about this one time, so I know what I'm talking about.) Then one day Mom refused to even go into the backyard and I knew we were just one step away from becoming a documentary ourselves: the woman who stays in bed all day and her son who has to do EVERYTHING.

That's when I knew I had to get Susie involved. *More* involved, that is. She came over right away. Susie is very dependable like that. Mom should think herself lucky. Some of us would kill to have a friend like that. (Ang and I still weren't talking.) She came breezing into the house, barking orders and being very un-Susie-like. She pulled back curtains and opened windows and picked up a series of half-empty teacups from around the place. She found two sitting on the windowsill.

"Thinking of starting a penicillin factory?" she said, thrusting the mugs at me, as if this was all my fault.

I stared into the mugs. The surface of the liquid was covered in an impressive lumpy, blue mold. Cool.

"Come on, now, wash," Susie barked.

I hid one of the mugs in the cupboard under the sink. No point in throwing out perfectly good mold.

When I'd finished washing the dishes, Susie handed me the vacuum and said, "Go ahead. Clean. You live here too, you know."

Oh, thank you for that revelation, I wanted to say to her,

because I had no idea where I lived. But I didn't because
Susie (bossy or not) was the best chance Mom and I had.
Though I did hope she'd go a bit easier on Mom, because I
didn't think she was up to being barked at. I didn't need to
worry.

"Let's go for a quick walk around the block," she said
gently to Mom, "just to get some air."

"I can't," Mom said.

"Yes, you can," Susie said. "I'll come with you."

"I can't," Mom said again.

Then she pulled off her bandanna and sat there with her
bald head. (She could hardly sit there without it, but you
know what I mean.)

Nobody said anything.

"Can I come too?" I said, just to break the silence. They
ignored me, but I didn't let it bother me. I get that a lot.
I just said, "We could go to the park."

"I am not going out," Mom said. "How can I?" Her voice
sounded like she didn't have enough air to speak. "Look at
me. *Look!*"

She rolled her bandanna into a ball and threw it at Susie.
Then she just sat there sobbing and howling and Susie told
her to go ahead and let it all out. To tell you the truth, I
didn't think it would do Mom any harm to keep some of it
in. All that emotion was wearing her out. And me.

Have you ever seen *Jurassic Park*? Remember the noise
the *Tyrannosaurus rex* makes when it gets injured, just
before it dies? Well, the noise my mom made that day

seriously resembled the cry of a dying dinosaur. She could get a job as a dinosaur voice double any day. Impressive. And scary.

Susie went over and sat beside her and tried to convince her that things weren't so bad, but Mom wasn't listening.

"I am not going out. People will see. People will know," she sobbed.

"Is that so bad?" Susie said. When Mom didn't answer, Susie lifted the traveling bag she'd brought with her and said, "All right, then, if you won't go out, we'll stay in." And she pulled out her pajamas and a bottle of wine. "Wine sleepover," she announced.

"Have you forgotten?" Mom said. "I can't drink."

"No, but I can," Susie said with a laugh. "You can watch. Just like the old days, when you were pregnant with Junior here."

"This isn't the old days," Mom said in this depressingly depressing voice.

So much for PMA, I thought, and left them to it.

I went upstairs and locked myself in the bathroom. I didn't have to go to the toilet. I just wanted to be in a room where no one could come barging in and tell me to do something. I sat on the toilet (lid down, pants up) and racked my brains trying to think of what I could do to help.

The phrase "Desperate times call for desperate measures" kept swimming around in my head. Our history teacher, Mr. Ross, had been overusing the phrase a lot in reference to our low marks. He claims it originates from Guy Fawkes, but I think he's just making that up, because what is the point of a desperate measure that's more desperate than the desperate problem? Guy Fawkes ended up dead, you know, minus his … head. And that's when I came up with my amazingly brilliant, incredibly genius (and a little bit scary) idea.

I stood in front of the bathroom mirror and braced myself. The pink plastic felt sweaty in my hand. I pressed the on switch and the razor buzzed into life. I touched it to my head and instantly recoiled. It was deafening. But I had to do this. There was no other choice, so I clenched my teeth and eyes really tight and put the screaming razor to my head again. Then I realized I had my eyes closed. A boy could lose an ear that way.

When I saw that the first glide had not left me bloodied and dying, I knew I could do it. It took ages. Even though my hair is really short, I kept having to stop and clean out clogged-up hair from the blades. I used the same tactic I use when Mom makes me cut the grass: I went around twice, making sure I'd gotten all the stray bits and had a good, smooth finish. The result wasn't exactly what I'd been aiming for. I looked a bit deranged, a cross between a slow loris and a psycho killer, because my eyes seemed bigger than usual, oversized, like they didn't fit my face anymore.

I stared at the scary bald kid in the mirror. He stared back at me.

"Here's to you, Harry Hill," he said. "This better work."

Then I slipped into my room, pulled on a woolly hat, and climbed into bed.

Dear Harry Hill,
I'm sorry I haven't written in ages. Being miserable is very time-consuming, you know. Anyway, I'm just writing to let you know that I've shaved my head too and with my new glasses on, I look like a mini you! Cool or what?

Yours sincerely,
Philip Wright

PS: Could you let me know where you buy those big-collared shirts you wear?

23
MYLIFEISNOT
ANACTIONMOVIE

THE MORNING AFTER I'd shaved my head, I got up early and left for school before Mom was even out of bed. I slipped out of the house, leaving her a note saying I had an early sports practice and had to be at school before eight. I had to get out; I couldn't risk her seeing me. Not yet.

"You look weird," Ang said to me as I grabbed some books from my locker. I wondered if he meant woolly-hat weird or bald-under-your-woolly-hat weird, but I didn't stop to ask him.

It was nearly break time before I was told to take the hat off. Wearing hats in class is forbidden, apparently. So is wearing no hair. We were in art at the time. Miss Franks said, "What's with the tea cozy, Philip?" and everyone had a laugh at my expense, but I didn't care. I had to do this. I guess Miss Franks thought that her tea cozy joke would make me take my hat off, but when it didn't, she just left me to it. Then Mr. Hinds, head of discipline, came in with a message for her. He spotted me right away.

"Stand up," he said.

And although he didn't name any names, we all knew

he meant me. He fixed me with a beady stare. I read somewhere that rodents do that just before they kill their prey. I
saw Mr. Hinds as a giant rat, whiskers twitching and glassy
eyes staring, and I felt sweat trickle down the back of my
shirt. My head itched like mad. It is impressively warm inside a genuine Norwegian hand-knitted pom-pom hat with
a snowflake design. I suppose on the fjords in Norway you
can't take any risks with the cold, but in an art classroom
considerably closer to the equator, the heat was excessive.
Little beads of sweat leaked down the side of my face.

"Hat, off," Mr. Hinds said.

I stared at him. Please no, not now. Any class but this.

Please, not in front of The Goddess.

"Now," Mr. Hinds said. You could tell he was getting a
bit peeved with me, because he was starting to overheat too.
His face had gone all tomato-y.

"Philip," Miss Franks said, trying to intervene, but Mr.
Hinds stopped her.

"I am going to count to three, and then I want you to
take off that ridiculous hat," he said in a voice that was very
final.

Ridiculous, huh? Norwegian knitwear manufacturers
would have something to say about that.

"One," Mr. Hinds said, and the entire class put down
their pencils and paintbrushes and art stuff to watch. You
could practically see the silence ripple around the room.

Everyone's eyes were on me.

If I didn't take the hat off, Mr. Hinds would frog-march
me to the principal and I'd be forced to take it off there.

And if I *did* take the hat off in class, I'd still be marched to the principal afterward. I was in for some serious punishment and humiliation, or some serious humiliation and punishment. It was really just a matter of which order I preferred. If I waited until we got to the principal's office, I would spare myself an excruciating scene in front of The Goddess, but I would also be buying myself a great big ugly grudge from Mr. Hinds. And he didn't get that job as head of discipline for nothing, you know.

"Two," Mr. Hinds said, and someone behind me gasped. In the end I figured it was only a matter of time before I had my humiliating moment with The Goddess. As soon as this hat came off it wouldn't be long before every single, solitary person in the school knew. So I decided I had nothing to lose, and just as Mr. Hinds got to three I put my hand up and pulled off the hat.

I say pulled it off, but actually it felt like I dragged it off in slow motion. The hush of the class and the drama of the moment and my own desperate fear made it seem like it was a scene from a movie where they cut the sound and slow the film right down, just for a minute, just before a big explosion. I half expected a motorcycle to come crashing through the window and save me, seconds before the hat finally came off.

But my life is not an action movie and a motorcycle did not come through the window. Instead the room was filled with gasps and squawks and hoots of laughter. Mr. Hinds was apoplectic. His complexion went from tomato to plum in a second. Boy, was I in for it!

I didn't dare move, but I could see Ang out of the corner of my eye. He'd risen from his seat and was moving toward Lucy, who was probably having a good sneer.

"*Quiet!*" Mr. Hinds bellowed, and pointed me to the door.

As I left, I turned to see Ang and Holly the Meerkat standing on either side of Lucy. And you know what? She wasn't sneering at me. She was crying.

24
RULES**IS**RULES

THE SCHOOL CALLED MOM at 11:15 a.m. and she was in the principal's office by noon. My plan had worked: I had forced Mom to leave the house. And, yes, she did still have three layers of disguise piled on her head, but it was a start.

Mom stared at my bald head, dumbstruck.

"I may have no option but to suspend Philip," the principal said. "We have a strict dress code: no shaved heads."

I think he was just saying that to try to provoke a response from Mom. I mean, what good would suspension do me? It wasn't like my hair would grow back in three days—that's the max I'd ever heard of anyone being suspended. Then I wondered if maybe he meant he was going to suspend me until my hair grew back. Cool, no school for months. But then I thought, not cool—months of being at home alone with Mom.

"Mrs. Wright?" the principal said. "The rules ..."

Mom still didn't say anything. She just stood there like a dumb animal. No offense meant—there are many handsome and majestic dumb animals out there. Only Mom wasn't at all majestic. It is hard to look anything other than downright silly (not to mention overdressed) when you're wearing a wig *and* a scarf *and* a hat.

The principal sighed and shifted uncomfortably in his seat.

Apparently there is a condition where people become mute for no biological reason. (Yes, I do watch too much TV.) Well, I figured Mom had developed the condition. She had not uttered one single sound since she'd come into the principal's office. She just kept staring at me with big watery eyes.

For a moment I was terrified. *Please God, NO!* I would drop dead there and then if she did her *Tyrannosaurus rex* impersonation. I considered falling down on my knees and begging her not to cry, but then I realized that her watery eyes weren't empty and desolate like the day before, when she was howling at Susie; they were sort of sad and happy, and oddly proud-looking, all at the same time.

"I take it you didn't know about this?" the principal said, trying to fill the enormous, gaping void left by Mom's silence. He was beginning to sound a bit desperate. "Mrs. Wright?"

And then ... you will never in a million, in a trillion years guess what happened next, so I am just going to come right out and tell you: *my* mom, the impressively silent Mrs. Kathleen Mary Joanna Wright, put her hand to her head and took off her hat. And then her head-scarf. And then, her wig.

She reached a hand toward me, and the two of us stood

there before the principal, silent and bald and smiling. It was the principal's turn to be struck dumb. The look on his face was priceless. I wish Ang could have been there to see it.

Miraculously, Mom's power of speech returned pretty swiftly after that.

"I have cancer," she said, plain and simple.

And I know this might sound a bit odd, but I felt really proud of her.

I didn't get detention or suspension or anything. In fact, Mom and I got a cup of tea in the school's good china cups in the principal's office. They were white with blue flowers on them, the kind of cups old ladies drink from. You'd think a principal would have something a bit more manly than that, wouldn't you?

Anyway, never mind the teacups; I learned something else that day. You know how people say "Good news travels fast"? Well, guess what? *Bad* news travels even faster. The news of my bald head and Mom's cancer was all over the school by lunchtime. The principal said that I could go home for the rest of the day, but I figured the worst that could happen already had.

And then I met The Yeti.

As usual, he was slow on the uptake. I think he hears things through a special filter, like a phone line breaking up so that instead of hearing "Philip Wright shaved his head because his mom has cancer," he heard, "Wright ... shaved ... head ... cancer." Then he put it all together, in the wrong order.

He walked right up to me and said, "There's nothing funny about cancer. You wouldn't like it if someone made fun of you."

And then he punched me in the stomach. Really hard. Really, really hard. I keeled over and started choking like an eighty-pound weakling. (I really need to bulk up.) Within seconds a crowd had gathered, but instead of shouting "Fight, fight!" they were solemn and silent.

"Cancer," somebody whispered, and they all turned and gave The Yeti the evil eye. Even Lucy.

The Yeti got a suspension. Apparently shaving your head trumps punching someone in the guts. There is a lesson to be learned there. I think.

Dear Harry Hill,

Don't you just love chaos theory? You know I told you I shaved my head? Well, the domino effects were astounding. Mom started going out again, the principal gave me a cup of tea, Lucy "The Goddess" Wells started smiling at me, and my bully got a suspension. Apparently he thought I was making fun of people with cancer, so he punched me. I am now very confused about the big oaf. I hate him for beating me up, but I am impressed by his impulse to defend cancer sufferers everywhere. Ain't life weird.

Yours sincerely,
Philip Wright

25
MRS. ANGRY

"THINGS ARE GOING TO CHANGE around here,"
Mom said, brandishing a duster at me.

I didn't like the sound of that. I'd shaved my head to
make things go back to the way they were. I didn't want
more change. I'd had enough of that already, thank you
very much.

But things did change. For starters, Susie moved in. She
came over one day with a big box of her stuff.

"It's only temporary," she said. "Just until you're on your
feet."

I knew I'd done a remarkable and inspiring thing (thank
you) getting Mom out of the house but I wasn't sure I could
keep it up and I had a terrible suspicion that we had a long
way to go yet, so Susie moving in was great. She got to
work on Mom, planning out each week and each day, each
hour. Every little bit of Mom's time was mapped out: sleeping, reading, exercise, food. It was really weird, like Mom
was learning how to live again.

Once Mom had gotten some kind of rhythm back (getting up during the day and sleeping at night like a normal,
non-vampire parent), she had more energy. Unfortunately,

she decided to pour her newfound energy into being angry. Luckily she was angry about "things" and not about me, but still, you had to be careful. If you disagreed with Mom she was liable to bite your head off, and if you agreed with her she was just as likely to bite your head off (apparently for "just humoring" her).

"There is nothing for cancer patients in this no-horse town," she said one day over tea. She had her angry voice on again.

"Hmm," Susie said. (This was her preferred method of dealing with Mom when she was in Angry Mode.)

"Well, I am going to change that," Mom said, banging her cup down on the table.

"Hmm." (Susie again)

"It's not good enough. The big towns and cities get all the help and we get what?" She didn't wait for an answer. "Zilch, nada, *NOTHING*! That's what we get. Well, I'm going to fix that."

"Hmm," Susie said again, but this time she creased her forehead and looked sideways, first at Mom, then at me.

"How are you going to do that?" I asked.

"I am going to set up my own cancer help group," Mom said.

Susie choked on her tea and spluttered a spray of liquid across the kitchen table.

"It's time someone around here did something," Mom said, getting all fired up. "I'm going to set up a support group that gives information and help and ..."

"All by yourself?" I asked.

"All by myself," Mom said. Her face was all flushed red and sort of holy-looking.

Good old Mom. Patron saint of cancer victims.

Honestly? I thought the idea was totally nutty (I really was "just humoring" her), so there was no need for Susie to shoot me that look which screamed, *Shut up, you fool*. I know Susie was worried that Mom would exhaust herself, but I didn't really think she should worry too much. Like Mom said, this is a no-horse town; where did she think she was going to get all these cancer victims to support? She'd be lucky to find more than one or two.

I was wrong. Apparently one in three people gets cancer. Our house was inundated. I came home from school one Wednesday afternoon to find the living room crowded with women.

"Oops," I said to Mom. "Sorry, I didn't know you had visitors." And then I saw them. Twenty assorted women, all wearing wigs or bandannas, or in Mom's case just sporting a bald head.

"Why don't you make us all a nice pot of tea?" Mom said. What did she think I was? I would've needed an industrial-size teapot and two whole boxes of cookies to go around.

"I've got homework to do," I said, backing out of the room.

I went upstairs and lay down on my bed. This was not the kind of development I had hoped for when I shaved my head. I just wanted things to be normal. I wanted Mom to be normal. I knew she could never "un-have" cancer, but

I didn't want to have to think about it all the time. It was boring. And depressing.

It wasn't long before I heard a knock at my door. Mom must have made the tea herself, because she had a mug for me and an iced cupcake on a saucer.

"Store-bought," she said and smiled.

I took the cupcake and swallowed it in two bites.

"You never wolf down my cupcakes like that," she said.

"Your cupcakes provide an aerobic workout for the jaw. It takes about twenty minutes to chew through the outer crust."

"The girls would like to meet you," she said, dropping all pretense of cupcake chat.

"No."

"They've heard all about you."

"No."

"They think of you as a hero."

"No," I said, but I could feel myself starting to weaken.

"You're something of a celebrity."

How is a boy supposed to resist the lure of celebrity? I could just see their adoring smiles.

"No," I said.

But this time Mom knew she'd won.

"I've told them you're a brilliant comedian," she said. "And we could do with cheering up. It's pretty heavy droning on about cancer all afternoon. We need some fun."

So she wasn't enjoying all this cancer business. That was a relief.

"You're just the man for the job," she said, rising to go.

"I am," I said. You can't argue with the truth.

"You could wear those silly Harry Hill look-alike glasses you and Susie bought when I was in the hospital."

"I could," I said.

"So you'll come down? Just for five minutes?"

"I think it'll take a lot longer than that. I have a bunch of new material to try out."

I decided to start with that animal joke about the horse who walks into a bar and the barman says, "Why the long face?" They were bound to love that.

I pulled off my Norwegian pom-pom hat, put on my glasses, and went downstairs to meet "the girls." When they saw me they gasped. Mom was right: they did think I was a celebrity. Excellent. I cleared my throat and began.

"Did you hear the one about ..."

"Wait," one of "the girls" said. (She was about seventy, so calling her a girl really was a bit of a stretch.) "Wait just one second; I need to get comfy."

Then she put down her teacup and took off her wig.

"Aha!" someone else said and took her wig off too.

And then the rest of them nodded their approval and did the same! And I was surrounded by a roomful of baldies.

"Now we all look a bit like Harry Hill," I said.

Mom coughed and shot me a disapproving look. What? What's not to like about Harry Hill?

"He's right, you know, we do," someone said and started giggling.

And once she'd started, she couldn't stop. And then the woman beside her joined in and pretty soon they were laughing away like hyenas.

And so, our very own Harry Hill Appreciation Society was born.

Dear Harry Hill,
Did you know that a side effect of chemotherapy is that it makes everyone look like a weird version of you? I know this for a fact because a crowd of Mom's cancer friends have started coming around to our house and when they take their wigs and scarves off, they all look a bit like you. Even the ones who don't wear glasses. So if you ever have chemotherapy you will have nothing to worry about because you will look just like yourself. Isn't that good to know?

I also thought you might like to know that I have gotten my comic genius back. I have been performing every week for Mom's friends. They think I'm hilarious. Which I am. They call themselves the Harry Hill Appreciation Society (on account of all the bald heads and the jokes) and they're planning a big fundraising bash to raise money to renovate an old camper van and turn it into a mobile cancer help unit for rural areas and no-horse towns like ours.

You will notice that I have written you a

longer letter than usual this time, and that is because I really need your help. Mom is expecting me to go on stage at this fundraiser bash and entertain the crowd, and I was wondering if maybe you could help me out with some new material. The cancer women have heard all my stuff already. Write soon, the fundraiser is in a few weeks. Actually, it might be better if you phone; our number is 288-976-5432.

Yours sincerely,
Philip Wright

26
FAIRGROUND ATTRACTION

I REALLY LOVED THE WHOLE FUNDRAISING,
camper-van, cancer-road-trip thing.

One of the women's husbands donated his ancient
camper van (a bit like Scooby-Doo's) and somebody else
knew somebody who knew a handyman who said he could
fix it up for us. Admit it, you have always wanted to live
in a camper van. Think of it: the tiny sink; the miniature
fridge that can hold only a quart of milk and one egg; the
bed doubling up as table doubling up as seat. And the
freedom to go wherever you want. Except our camper van
couldn't go anywhere on account of it only having three
tires and missing an engine.

We got to keep it in our driveway until it was fixed and
I was allowed to go in and hang around in it anytime I
wanted. And the best part was that I sometimes saw Ang
looking jealously at the van from across the street. I bet he
wished we were best buddies now. Well, tough. He chose
The Yeti; I chose "the crazy camper-van project."

There was one big problem with the project: it required
money. Everyone gave what they could, but even I knew it

would never be enough, so we all sat around thinking up ways of raising money.

After some very uninspired suggestions like a sponsored knit-athon (no way) and a sponsored silence (yawn), someone came up with the idea of a "cancer fun day." I thought putting the words "cancer" and "fun" in the same sentence was not clever, but I was alone in thinking this because everyone else latched on to the idea and said, "Yes, let's have a fun day!"

What do ya know!

So we all started talking about how we could hire the community hall for the day and have lots of games and treats.

"We could have a dunk tank," someone said.

"And a ring toss."

"And cotton candy."

"And cream-pie throwing," I suggested. I pictured The Yeti covered in gloop.

"And a make-your-own-smoothie corner," said some-one else.

"Good idea. And healthy-eating stalls."

"And unhealthy-eating stalls. Marge here makes a mean cheesecake."

The ideas kept coming. One of the women, it turned out, was a yoga instructor and she offered to give free lessons.

Another described herself as a "nail technician." I thought that meant she manufactured nails and screws for a living, but apparently not. She does women's nails and she has some really wacky designs, like spiderwebs. Everyone thought it was a great idea, so I went along with it. What do I know about women's nails?

Then one woman who didn't speak very often piped up and said she was an archery expert, and if the weather was good she could set up some target practice on the lawn outside the hall. Awesome.

There was only one dodgy moment, when someone suggested a cancer information desk and some kind of cancer screening booth. She had obviously lost the plot. It was supposed to be a *fair*. We were supposed to have *fun*, so I said, "Wrong time, wrong place. We want people to eat cotton candy and throw cream pies at each other, not run screaming from a booth because they've just found out they have cancer."

There was a terrible silence while everyone stared at me.

Then the oldest one in the group said, "Ah, the wisdom of youth."

They all nodded in agreement and went back to talking about sensible things like face painting and a balloon man for the little kids and a raffle and a DJ.

Then Susie suggested a costume contest. I hate costumes. My deep-seated hatred stems from that time when Mom sent me to a costume day in elementary school dressed as a schoolboy. She called it irony. I called it excruciating. I think I must have groaned out loud at the costume idea because Mom caught my eye and gave me one of her looks.

Then she said, "OK, scrap that Harry Hill costume idea."

"Fine," Susie said. "It was only a thought."

"Hang on," I said. "Harry Hill?"

And within minutes, with a majority show of hands and a lot of grinning, it was agreed that the fun day would have a costume: everyone should come dressed as Harry Hill—black suit, big glasses, bald head, and all. Genius.

And the best part?

Everyone agreed that, as well as the DJ, we would need some live entertainment: a comic performer to act as master of ceremonies (that's fancy for host). And who better than—*ME*!

Oh my God! This could be my big break.

27
FEVERPITCH

TWO WEEKS before the big fundraising bash, Mom was rushed to the hospital. Luckily Susie was still staying with us because it all happened in a panic in the middle of the night when Mom woke with a raging fever and couldn't stop throwing up. I stared at her horrified as she vomited into a bucket at the side of the bed. I patted her shoulder stupidly a few times because I couldn't think of anything else to do. She winced under my hand. I couldn't tell if she was wincing because I was getting on her nerves or because that slight touch was hurting her; either way, it wasn't good, so I stopped.

Susie called the doctor from the bedroom phone and an ambulance came immediately. All they would say was that Mom had a fever (duh!) and that it was worrying. I thought that was ridiculous because I've had a fever plenty of times and I've never been rushed to the hospital because of it. So it was obvious that they were lying to me.

"They're lying," I said to Susie. "You're lying. People don't go to the hospital just because they have a fever."

"Cancer patients do," Susie said, trying to calm me down. "It's just routine."

"No, it's not. It's not routine. If it was routine it would be in all those cancer leaflets Mom litters the house with. 'Week 15: go to the hospital with a fever.'"

We were standing outside the hospital ward at the time. They wouldn't let us in because they were "settling" Mom in. She didn't need them to settle her in; I could've done that. I could have tucked in her sheets and put her stuff in the bedside locker. I could have set out her picture of me sitting on Grandpa Joe's knee—the picture she kept beside her bed at home. That would have settled her. I could have laid out her lipstick and that tiny mirror she carries around in her bag "for emergencies." They didn't know how vain Mom was. They didn't know anything about her. They didn't know that she only liked one pillow because she got a crick in her neck if she used two. They didn't know that she takes her tea with just the right amount of milk—the color of digestive cookies, *not* the color of shortbread. They didn't know that she likes to sleep in full, unspeaking darkness, the kind of darkness that made a little kid stub his toe on the doorjamb when he wandered into her room in the middle of the night, needing her.

They didn't know anything.

"What do they know!" I yelled at Susie and thumped the door to the ward with my fist. Really hard; hot pain shot through it.

Susie stepped back, shocked. Then she took my hand and said, "You're right. This is serious. We just have to wait."

And then we just stood there gawping at each other like

two people who were lost on the moon without a map.

When a nurse finally came to talk to us, she said Mom was asleep and shouldn't be disturbed. We'd have to come back tomorrow.

I didn't sleep. Neither did Susie. I could hear her in the spare room, twisting and turning and sighing. At about three in the morning, when the house was still and I assumed Susie was dozing, I slipped out of bed and crept into Mom's room. I didn't put the light on. The duvet was rumpled up in a big mound, pushed to one side. In the dark you could almost think she was still there.

I sat on the edge of the bed and laid my hand on the mound of duvet.

Then I whispered into the darkness, "It's all right, Mom. You're going to be all right."

Aren't you?

Then I got up and wrote to Harry Hill.

Dear Harry Hill,

Mom was taken to the hospital because she has a fever that she can't get rid of and she looks awful and the doctors won't talk to me because I'm too young. So I thought, with your medical background, you might be able to tell me if she's going to be all right. She has a temperature of 104 and is vomiting. Is that normal? Do you think she'll be better in time for the fundraising fair, which is two weeks away?

You can ignore all the stuff in my other letters if you want, but this one is deadly important. Please write back quickly.

Yours sincerely,
Philip Wright

PS: Can you die from a fever?

28
DOCTORDOCTOR!

WHEN THEY FINALLY LET US IN to see Mom the next afternoon, she looked awful. Really awful. Susie burst into tears when she saw her, which was seriously unhelpful. And all I could think of was Grandpa Joe, which wasn't much help either, since he was dead.

Have you ever seen a dead person in real life? Well, not in real life because then they wouldn't be dead, they'd be alive. I mean a dead person in reality, not on TV. I have. I saw Grandpa Joe laid out in his coffin when he died. The coffin was open so that you could go in and keep him company if you wanted. Weird, but kind of nice too.

Anyway, I couldn't help thinking of Grandpa Joe like that because Mom's skin was the same waxy yellow his was when he died, like all the blood had been drained out. I'm not trying to be melodramatic here; I'm just telling you what I saw.

I desperately wanted to give Mom a hug but I couldn't because of all the drips and tubes and things, so I just gave her a little peck on the cheek. Her skin felt cold but it was sticky and there were tiny beads of perspiration on her face. So that is what is meant by a cold sweat. I thought it was just something English teachers made up to explain what a paradox is.

Mom smiled at me and pursed her lips in a kiss but she didn't lift her head from the pillow. She said it felt too heavy. A ton weight, she said. Her voice was all whispery and worn out. Instead, she just reached her hand out to me and I sat there holding it. It was sweaty and cold too.

Susie stood behind me and said nothing but I could tell she was crying even though she was trying to pretend she wasn't. I could hear her breathing catch. None of us had anything to say.

After what seemed like two nanoseconds the nurse came and told us to leave. Mom was tired, she said. I didn't want to go and I must have started making a fuss because Susie had to put her arm around me and pull me away from the bed. I hated myself then because Mom looked really upset.

Then I realized she wasn't upset with me, because she lifted her hand and beckoned me back. I leaned in close and felt her breath on my face. It was warm and weak. "Tell me a joke," she said. "I love you … telling me jokes."

She stumbled on the words.

I thought a "Doctor, doctor" one seemed appropriate, so I told her the one about the man who goes to see the doctor with a banana in his ear and a cucumber up his nose.

She was asleep before I got to the end of it.

A nurse coughed and came to check Mom's drip. She pressed some buttons on the monitor and said, "That's better, Kathleen, isn't it?"

And even though her voice was kind, I hated her. My mom's name is Kathy. Not Kathleen. No one calls her Kathleen. No one but me, when I'm teasing and pretending to boss her around.

The nurse turned to me. "Mom needs to rest," she said in her soft, sticky voice.

Don't call her Mom, I wanted to yell. *She's not your mom.*

But I didn't. I just sat there holding Mom's hand and ignored the nurse.

"It's time to go," the nurse said, looking to Susie for help.

"Philip?" Susie said.

I ignored her too. What I really wanted to do was climb up on Mom's bed and lie there beside her, but the big BOLD-face sign telling relatives *NOT* to lie on the beds put me off.

I will never be a hero. Heroes don't heed signs like that. Heroes just plow on and do something heroic. Not me, I am a very obedient person. Biddable, Grandpa Joe used to always say.

But just then, I would not be bidden. I would not move. I pulled the chair up close and laid my face on the pillow beside Mom and let her feel my breath on her cheek. She seemed to be barely breathing, like no air was getting in or out because she didn't have the strength to make it.

I moved my head closer, put my lips to her ear, and breathed in. And I know it was stupid but I just had to do it. I had to breathe some life into her.

I don't remember leaving the ward or the drive home

from the hospital. I don't remember Susie making me hot chocolate or fixing me a hot water bottle or tucking me into bed like a baby, though she later swore she did.

I do remember lying in my bed thinking of Grandpa Joe. I saw him stiff in his coffin, yellow and cold. Dead. Not coming back. Not ever.

Mom was that same color, and almost as still. What if she didn't come back? What then? Whose kiss would I duck then, whose soft nagging would I ignore? Who would know to leave my gym bag at the front door on phys ed day because I have "a head like a sieve"? Who would know that I like my eggs on toast *off* the toast, that I like sugar in iced tea but not in hot tea, that I have a slight intolerance to milk? (It makes me farty.) Who would ruffle my hair (so seriously annoying) and ask, "How was your day?" and genuinely want to hear the answer?

And even if someone, Susie, anyone, could learn all this, even if Mom could write a guide and leave it—"An A–Z of Philip Wright"—it would still be all wrong. That person, that "replacement," would be all wrong. They would feel wrong and smell wrong and move wrong. They would sound wrong and think wrong. They would *breathe* wrong. I could not live in that wrong world. Mom had to come back. She had to.

And so I lay there in the middle of the bed curled up in a ball and I cried out, "Come back! Come back! Mom, *please come back!*"

Dear Harry Hill,
I want you to know that my outlook on life will never be the same again—I'll never be able to admire my heroes again. And it's all your fault.

How could you? You go on TV and are all nice and funny and friendly. You sometimes even have ordinary people on your show. But really, you don't care about ordinary people like me or Mom.

Would one letter have killed you?

This is the last time I will ever write. I've had it with you.

Goodbye,
Philip Wright

29
THE BEST MEDICINE

YOU KNOW HOW people sometimes say they nearly peed themselves with anxiety or excitement, just to be funny? Well, I can tell you it's not one bit funny. On the day of the fair my nerves were wrecked and I kept wanting to pee and we ended up arriving late.

Not just because of me—it was Susie's fault, really. She was driving, but she made us all late talking to someone on the phone about something to do with the fair that was "none of my business." She seemed to have forgotten that I was the host and the star attraction. And the star attraction's nerves couldn't take much more of this.

And then when we did finally get there Mom refused to be pushed around in a wheelchair, so I had to sit with her instead of getting ready backstage. I don't understand Mom—I've always wanted to break my legs and get spun around in a wheelchair. I thought everyone did. People kept coming up and hugging her and saying she looked great, which was really kind because she didn't look great; she looked sick. But seeing the fair put a smile on her face. *Anyway,* I had to sit there "watching" her and Mrs. Chihuahua, who'd come along in Susie's car. (Note: savage, smelly Chihuahua, three adults, and one boy in a compact car is not a good combo.) Meanwhile, Susie dashed around talking to people on her cell like she was the important one here.

PMA, I told myself—at least we had good seats. We could see everything: the streamers and balloons and colored lights and pictures of Harry Hill all around the walls; the stalls with food and drink and games and demonstrations; and the *dozens* of Harry Hills. There were so many bald wigs and big black glasses it was difficult to tell who was who, but I definitely saw Ang and his mom and dad over at the ring toss, and I'm fairly sure I saw Lucy and her meerkat friend Holly having their nails painted by the nail technician woman. There was a crowd of others from school too, and they were all in bald wigs. I even saw the principal and, unbelievably, Mrs. Gray, who came up and said hello and didn't mention poetry once. And she was wearing a bald wig too!

Then I spotted a woman carrying a large camera taking a bunch of pictures. Mom had said journalists would be coming. Think of it: the Harry Hill Appreciation Society would be in the paper! I'd be famous.

"Do you think they'll have us splashed all over the front page?" I said.

"Maybe they will," Mom said with a grin.

And then a little kid ran in, squealing something about more cameras and men and I don't know what else, because just at that minute the DJ played a big blast of Harry Hill music, which meant I was about to be introduced onstage.

Except I wasn't on stage or backstage or side stage, and before I could get past Mrs. Casey and her humongous knitting bag, which she'd brought with her "just in case," the lights went out and the DJ started introducing me.

"Ladies and gentlemen," he said, "please put your hands together for our host today."

I seriously thought I was going to faint or choke or explode or implode or something. (Not sure I know the difference between those last two.) I would look like an idiot when the curtains opened and I wasn't there, except no one would see idiot me, but you know what I mean. This was a disaster. I tried waving frantically at the DJ but he didn't even notice. He just went on doing his introduction. And he was clearly loving it because he kept dragging it out: "Ladies and Gentlemen . . . let me introduce . . . your host today . . . "

And then he cranked the music up some more and the curtains opened. And there onstage was the real—the *actual*—Harry Hill.

The crowd went wild, and I very nearly peed myself.

Luckily, I have exceptional bladder control because the next thing that happened was that Harry Hill (yes, *the* Harry Hill) called me up on stage! I think you'll agree that pee-stained pants is not a good look on anyone, especially not someone who is invited onstage with a world-class comedian and who then spends a whole half hour entertaining everyone with a comic routine which *the* Harry Hill described as classic. Do you hear that? I am *classic*.

I played it safe and started with some animal jokes. You

can't go wrong with animals. People either love them and think the joke is cute or they hate animals and think it's OK to make fun of them. It's a win–win situation. After that, I moved on to a whole pile of "Doctor, doctor" jokes, and you know what? Harry Hill knew them all and actually joined in, so that I was the patient and he was the doctor and it was like we'd rehearsed it or something, and we were this brilliant, hilarious duo.

You know how people say you should never meet your heroes, because you'll be disappointed? Well, they are *so* wrong. Harry Hill was even nicer and even funnier in real life, and apart from the "Doctor, doctor" act, he hardly interrupted me at all when I was on stage.

After the performance, Harry Hill's "security people" swooped in around him and announced that he couldn't stay long, but he did sign some autographs (mostly on people's bald wigs), and then he sat down to talk to Mom. Wasn't that thoughtful? He could see she was still a bit too weak to be standing up in a crush of crazy autograph-hunting fans. It's probably his medical training. Or maybe he is just a nice guy, because he even had a little chat with old Mrs. Casey. He gave Alfred Pickles a pat on the head and said something funny about Paris Hilton and dogs in purses, but it was obvious Mrs. Casey hadn't the faintest idea what he was talking about. To tell you the truth, I'm still not convinced she even knew who Harry Hill was.

He told Mom I was a credit to her and said that I was really thoughtful, which was nice, because no one has ever called me thoughtful before. I really wished The Goddess had been there to hear that, but she was across the room gossiping with The Meerkats.

Once we were off stage, I got all starstruck and could barely say a word to Harry Hill. I had all these questions in my head that I'd stored up for years, but I couldn't get any out. I just sort of grunted, but Harry didn't seem to mind; he made a comment about me being shy, and said he had really enjoyed reading all my letters. He'd only gotten them a few weeks ago—all in one batch.

"They just kept piling up," he said. "I spotted them when I went in to the office to sign some documents one day. That's when I got on the phone to your mom."

He said my letters had really made him laugh, but I couldn't see how that could be the case, since they were an impassioned plea for help from a desperate child, not a string of jokes. But I didn't argue. All I could think about was that final, awful letter I'd written him. It just goes to show how heroic your heroes are when they can overlook a thing like that.

As he was leaving, Harry Hill kissed Mom on the cheek and she went red, and everyone burst out laughing. After he'd left, people couldn't stop smiling. Especially me and Mom. It was like he had cast a spell on us. In fact, the whole place was infected with a party atmosphere and no one wanted to go home. And just in case there was any danger of that, the DJ got up and told people not to even think about leaving because there was lots more entertainment.

Then he said, "Wow, ladies and gentlemen, Harry Hill! Can you believe it?" for about the sixtieth time.

"So," I said to Mom, "that's what Susie's 'private' phone calls were about."

I had to hand it to them. They could probably get jobs as spies or something. I could never in a million years have kept a secret that big.

"Group hug!" Susie squealed, bounding over toward us. And right there in public view she squished Mom and me into her arms.

Now, don't get me wrong, I could forgive nearly anything after arranging that whole Harry Hill surprise, but I did still sneak a look around the hall to see if anyone was watching us. And of course they were. Lucy and Ang and Holly the Meerkat were staring right at us. With big, stupid grins on their faces. Ang and Holly still had their bald wigs on, but Lucy was taking hers off and was shaking her goddess hair free. She looked lovelier than ever.

When they saw me looking over, all three started to come toward me. And for the second time that day I thought I was seeing things, only this time the whole thing was in slow-motion splendor, like one of those sappy parts in a movie.

Ang and Holly were walking slowly toward me. And they were holding hands!

"You and Holly!" I gasped.

"How could you not know, dude?" Ang said to me. "How could you not see?"

He turned to Holly and grinned at her like an idiot. The best idiot friend in the world.

I turned to Lucy. "So, not you and Ang?" I said.

"No!" she said and shook her incredibly beautiful head and laughed.

"So that just leaves you and Eddie Lyttle." I felt a bit sick just saying the words.

"Are you nuts!" Lucy said. "That's probably illegal or something. He's my cousin."

"Cousin?" I squealed, yes, *squealed*. I really must learn to master that impulse to sound like a strangulated mouse. It is *so* not cool.

"Yes. *Cousin*," Lucy said. "You'd know that if you ever stopped to listen, but you're too busy hating him. And you shouldn't because you actually have a lot in common."

Now, I may have resembled a love-struck poodle (a bald one) but I was not about to pretend that I had some kind of bond with The Yeti. I am neither fat, hairy, nor brainless.

"Yeah, right," I said.

"Yes, right," Lucy said, pointing across the room to where Holly and Ang had gone.

I didn't get it at first. Then I realized they were talking to The Yeti—but he wasn't The Yeti anymore. His hideous mane of hair was gone. And it wasn't hidden under a wig. He had shaved off all his hair. Just like me.

"That woman standing behind him with the blue bandanna is his mom," Lucy explained. "Auntie Claire. She has breast cancer too. Her hair is starting to grow back now and she says she looks like a hedgehog without her bandanna, so she kept it on."

I was speechless. So I just stood there. Speechless.

"Ha!" Lucy said, shaking her incredibly super-gorgeous

head. "Don't tell me the famous I've-swallowed-a-dictionary Philip Wright is at a loss for words?"

The famous Philip Wright just stood there like a dummy.

A very stupid dummy.

And then, as if I wasn't feeling stupid enough, Lucy said, "Honestly, Philip, you are so wrapped up in yourself, you don't even notice what's in front of your nose. Should we go over and talk to them?"

If my life were a cheesy, made-for-TV movie, I'd have said yes; we'd all embrace and The Yeti and I would become best friends and live happily ever after, possibly going into business together in adulthood as highly successful baldcap manufacturers.

But I don't live in a TV movie, so I said, "Not yet. I like it here."

And Lucy said, "Me too."

She nudged me with her elbow and giggled. "How could you not know that Ang and Holly were gaga for each other?"

I looked at her and shrugged. She stopped giggling and took a step closer to me. "How can you not see?" she said slowly.

And then—you are so seriously never going to believe this—Lucy slipped her hand into mine. And we stood there smiling, like two people who had just found the answer to everything.

Now, I don't want to go all philosophical and kill the mood, but you know how old people say *laughter is the best medicine* and you think no it's not, you can't laugh your way out of a bad case of athlete's foot? (Trust me, I know.) So, while I knew I wasn't going to actually cure anyone with jokes, the fact is that there were a lot of happy faces at that fair. The members of the Harry Hill Appreciation Society had never looked so good. They were shining with happiness. Even Mom. I hadn't seen her look this good in months. So there must be more than a grain of truth in that whole laughter-is-the-best-medicine thing.

Maybe I'll write to Harry Hill and see what he thinks.

30
ASHININGMOMENT

YOU'D THINK HAVING CANCER and surviving
chemotherapy and undergoing radiation therapy and
facing death and coming out the other side would mean
you wouldn't sweat the small stuff anymore, wouldn't you?
Well, you'd be wrong.

One day, after all Mom's treatments had ended and
they'd declared her well enough to go back to work, I came
home from school to find her clutching a black velvet dress
and crying, *bawling*, into it. Big fat tears ran down her
cheeks and splashed onto the velvet. They sat in unburst
blobs on the fabric.

I tried desperately to figure out what the dress could
symbolize, because it was clear to me that no one, not even
Mom, could get that upset over a piece of clothing. But I
couldn't figure it out, so I just put my arm around her and
said, "It's okay."

"It doesn't fit me anymore," she blubbed, and let out a
fresh wail of despair. "I can't go back to work in a tracksuit."

You'd think losing a boob would mean Mom would've
shed a pound or two, but the opposite was true. Part of the
problem was all those drugs they kept giving her. First they

160

gave her drugs that made her vomit all the time. Then they gave her drugs that made her really hungry. All the time. So she went on a diet. Quite a cranky diet, as it happened. Living on lettuce leaves and rice cakes does nothing for your mood. She only smiled if the scale said she'd lost weight, but the smile only lasted a few minutes and then she'd be back to lecturing me for waltzing around the house eating all the time. Which was unfair, because I don't waltz.

Poor Mom. I really wished she could lose some of that weight, because even though I've told her (and so has Susie) that it's a small price to pay for your life and what's the harm of a few pounds, I know that it matters to her. I know how vain and beautiful she was before all of this started. So in an attempt to help her lose weight, I started keeping my junk food stash in my closet, and together we ate sensible portions of lettuce leaves and cucumber, and the see-through diet soup that Mrs. Casey brought over, the main ingredients of which seemed to be water and onions. Apparently it had zero calories. It had zero taste as well, but I ate it anyway, just to keep Mom company.

Apart from Mom and her squishy tummy, which was clearly going to take some time to change, the rest of my life started to mend remarkably quickly. Ang and me just went back to being Ang and me. We didn't talk about it or think about it, or harp on about it, we just did it.

Lucy says that if Ang and I were girls we'd have had to talk it all through and analyze it and make promises and resolutions and say sorry before we could be reconciled. I am so glad I am not a girl. It must be exhausting thinking about stuff all the time. I prefer to keep my head empty. Much simpler.

And speaking of my head, my hair started to grow back and, much to Mom's relief, so did my grades and things seemed like they were really getting back on track. I even impressed Mrs. Gray one day. I had been making Ang laugh, so she moved me to the desk at the front of the class that she keeps for "dunderheads and loafers," and that's when this amazing and weird thing happened.

After I'd been moved, Mrs. Gray said we were going to do some poetry. I think that instead of announcing it, she should have just ambushed us, because as soon as she uttered the word "poem" everyone started talking and chucking scrunched-up balls of paper around and tapping their pens and groaning and making faces and gestures like they'd rather kill themselves than read a poem.

Anyway, she started handing out the poem and because I was at the front of the class at her dunderheads' desk, I got a copy of it first. And since I had absolutely no other form of entertainment available to me, I read it. It was about a boy peeling potatoes in the kitchen with his mother one Sunday morning when the rest of the family was out at church and they just worked in silence and their heads were together so that their breaths met. It was sort of magical, like a dream. But then in the second verse the boy was a man and his mother was dying and people were praying around her bedside and it was scary until he remembered that time peeling potatoes with her. As soon as I read the

poem, the weird thing happened: sounds from the classroom fell away, and it was like I was in a time machine or
something, where I could see my younger self—with Mom
hanging up laundry, and with Grandpa Joe hammering
nails in his shed. It was like watching a movie trailer for my
life with the sound turned down. All this from one solitary
poem! It was mind-blowing.

"So, folks," Mrs. Gray said, "in this poem, the poet is
writing about his mother, and it's on your end-of-semester
exam, so listen up. Who would like to read?"

You'd think someone of Mrs. Gray's professional matu-
rity would know by now that the answer to that question is
always no one.

"No one?" she said after a desperate look around the
bowed heads of the class. "OK, then, I will."

She started to read the poem aloud and one or two
people shut up to listen.

I wish I could remember it all to repeat the words here
but I can't and no way am I going to ask Mrs. Gray for a
copy. I'm one of those people who does actually learn from
their mistakes. Anyway, when she'd finished reading, Mrs.
Gray asked us what we thought it was about and nobody
answered, so she did what teachers always do in those cir-
cumstances: she started picking us out one by one.

"Ang?" she said.

"Potatoes?" Ang said hopefully and everyone laughed.

"Matthew? What do you think it's about?"

"Huh?" Matthew Brown said, without lifting his head

from the desk, where it was lying as if it was so heavy he needed a rest from carrying it around all day.

Mrs. Gray sighed.

"Fiona, what about you?"

"Dunno, Ma'am," Fiona said. "Is it about liking potatoes better than going to church?"

"Philip?" Mrs. Gray said in this really defeated voice.

"It's about memory," I said, "and love and loss."

"Oh!" Mrs. Gray said, looking startled. "Go on."

"It's about a man remembering time spent with his mother when he was a boy. Ordinary special time. When it was just the two of them and they peeled potatoes in silence and loved each other without having to say it. And then when she is dying, that memory comes back to him to take care of him and help him. And the memory of his mom shines out, and it is like a moment. A gleaming, golden moment. And that is what memories are, aren't they? Because even if someone dies and leaves you, you can never unknow them. You can never unhave them. They're yours forever and they can come back and help you in your memories when you need them."

I stopped. There was silence all around the room and everyone was staring at me, including Mrs. Gray. Her face was all flushed red, and she looked like she was in pain. So I figured I must have gotten this poem all wrong. "I think," I added, as if that would make me look less stupid.

Mrs. Gray blinked at me and turned away to wipe the board even though there was nothing written on it. "Philip, oh, gosh—very good," she said. "Very—excellent."

164

And even though her voice sounded funny, I think she meant it. "Excellent" is not a word Mrs. Gray likes to overuse.

When she turned back to the class, her voice and face were normal again.

"Now," she said, "can you all write down two examples of alliteration. That's two *L*s and one *T*." And that was that. My one "very excellent" moment in English was over.

31
YETIANOTHERDAY

SO THERE I WAS, making my way down to art class, when a thick hand landed on my shoulder. Eddie Lyttle. I froze and felt his fingers press into my still-feeble frame. I told myself I had nothing to be afraid of, but it didn't work; my breathing started to get all choked up and panicky. It felt like my Adam's apple had swollen to ten times its normal size and was pressing on my windpipe. Not cool. If I choked to death like that, there wouldn't be a court case because Eddie hadn't even done anything. There'd be no forensics, no inquest, no dramatic courtroom ending.

Eddie pressed down harder, then shook me to make me turn, and as I did, he shoved something sharp into my stomach.

"What's wrong with you?" he said.

When I didn't answer he shoved the sharp thing into my stomach again.

"Take that," he grunted.

Now, I don't care what Lucy says about him being "nice, really." He needs to speak more clearly if he wants to make friends. Grunting is very off-putting.

"Go ahead," he mumbled. "Take it."

I looked down and saw that he was shoving a book at me. Interesting murder weapon, there. Death by book. I looked at the cover; it had a picture of leaves and dried fruit on it. Wow. Maybe he was planning to bore me to death.

"It's a book," he said, shoving the book (hardcover, glossy, very pointy corners) into my gut again.

"Wow," I wanted to say, "a book-shaped book—who'd have guessed!" But I have turned over a new leaf. Lucy says that I can sometimes give the wrong impression and come across as a bit of a smart aleck. So I just said, "A book?"

"Yeah, dummy. A book," Eddie said. "Your mom asked my mom if she could borrow it. It's about eating healthy after cancer or losing weight or something."

And then I really was a dummy: The Yeti, Eddie Lyttle, my sworn enemy, was doing something nice for my mom. Not his own mom, *mine*. And, well, what was I meant to do in the face of such un-bullylike behavior?

"Thanks," I said. Not quite the articulate and heartrending speech of reconciliation you might have hoped for, but then we are teenage boys (almost), so what do you expect?

And he said, "No problem, man."

Man? Eddie Lyttle called me "man"!

And then he slapped me on the back and trudged off. Leaving me late for art.

NOTE

THE POEM REFERRED TO in Chapter 30 is from a
sonnet sequence by Seamus Heaney called "Clearances,"
which was voted Ireland's favorite poem of the last one
hundred years by listeners of RTÉ Radio (Ireland's national
broadcaster) in 2015. The sonnet has no title but is referred
to by its first line, "When all the others were away at Mass."
It was first published in *The Haw Lantern* (1987); it also
appears in Heaney's *New Selected Poems 1966–1987*, or you
can find it online.

ABOUT THE AUTHOR

CHRISTINE HAMILL lives with her son in Belfast,
Northern Ireland, and teaches creative writing at a college.
This is her first novel and her first book for youth. She is
also the author of a nonfiction book for adults, *B Is for
Breast Cancer*.